THEN THERE WAS YOU

NEW YORK TIMES BEST SELLING AUTHOR

CLAIRE CONTRERAS

THEN THERE WAS YOU

My readers, the ones who lifted me when my spirit was broken.

Thank you for waiting for me.

This one's for you.

I read our story to the moon
and even she split in half that night

JM. WONDERLAND

CHAPTER ONE

TESSA

IF YOU DIDN'T KNOW the Hawthorne boys, you probably weren't from around here. They were the center of attention even when attention wasn't warranted, like right then when Rowan, the oldest Hawthorne, was taking his usual morning jog. It would have just been a shirtless guy jogging, but Rowan made the thermometer on the hotness spectrum spill mercury with his looks. I'd always found him attractive, but the women in town decided there had been a turning point in which he'd gone from a really good-looking kid to a hot-as-hell man. And so, every morning, like clockwork, while I was lifting the last of the rolls of fabric into my truck and the moms were loading their minivans, for just a few short minutes, they stopped to watch Rowan.

It had only been two weeks since I'd been back in town, and I'd already stopped looking, but I could tell exactly the pattern in which the sweat dripped down his back and chest. I didn't even need to close my eyes to recount where the tiny birthmarks were on his broad shoulders. And I didn't need to delve that far into the past to tell you the way his blue eyes hazed and his Adam's apple bobbed when he was turned on. I didn't have to imagine any of it like some of those women did when they were with their own husbands. I'd had him once.

I hopped into the truck, slid the key into the ignition, and held my breath, praying that it would start. Last summer, when I'd been home for a month, I hadn't thought this thing would be around much longer. So, I was both surprised and disappointed when I'd come back for this short visit and found that it was still running . . . sort of.

It wasn't that I hated the truck, because I didn't. It was that the thought of the truck finally giving up the good fight acted as scissors to the one of last ties I had to this place. Again, it wasn't that I didn't love it here, it was that every time I visited, I felt like this place would threaten to suck me into a sinkhole and I'd be stuck for good. I wasn't even sure why I felt that way.

My brother Freddie left. My sister Celia left. Even my parents went their separate ways, though, they'd both come back to visit separately on occasion—Dad to check on the house; Mom to check on my grandmother. I was the last one left to pick up whatever things I wanted to put in storage, and I'd spent the last week working on that. It was down to clearing a few things out and listing the house, which we'd all agreed I'd do before I left unless I had to leave before I got a chance to. In that case, Grandma Joan would do it, but Dad really didn't want that. I knew that regardless of how badly I wanted to leave and never look back, I'd miss these streets and the lake and the memories.

The truck made another sound, as if it was just about to start, but didn't. I pounded on the dash for good measure. I'd turned down my grandmother's offer of driving the candy-apple-red corvette sitting in her driveway, a gift she bought herself a few years ago. The car had fewer than two thousand miles on it, which told me how little driving she actually did. I politely declined the offer and chose to drive the beat-up old truck parked outside of my childhood home instead. It was my grandfather's truck, then my father's, then Freddie's first car, then Celia's first car, and for a short time, mine. The truck had seen better days, but as long as it took me from point A to point B, I'd be fine.

Thankfully, after two questionable grunts and a love tap on the dash, the truck roared to life. I let out a relieved breath as I backed out, chancing a glance in the direction of the shirtless stranger. That was all he was to me anymore. A stranger.

Our eyes collided, and I felt my heart stall, as if to say, *"A stranger? You sure about that?"* I answered myself by lifting my chin and turning to focus on the road ahead.

In a few short weeks, I'd be out of here for good and wouldn't have to be subjected to his stupid little head games that made me wonder whether or not he was still interested in me. I'd be too busy with my apprenticeship in New York City or Paris. My pulse thrummed with possibilities. The apprenticeship, whichever one I took, was a dream, something I'd been working for my entire life. Something that was afforded to me because my parents made it possible for me to go to that fancy ivy league and because I'd worked my ass off once I'd gotten my foot in the door.

Soon, I'd be able to show them they hadn't thrown away their money, that they hadn't . . . my thoughts were cut off by a strange *tut-tut-tut* noise.

Oh shit.

I watched the speedometer, the needle dropping more with each *tut*, and gripped my steering wheel a little tighter as I took my foot off the accelerator. Letting the truck coast a little on its own, I tried not to focus on the pit of dread curling with a sick heat in my stomach.

Most of the dirt roads, aside from the ones behind our houses, were gone. This had always been my favorite and fastest route to the factories. With views of the water behind the tall trees and very few commuters to break behind. The land had been purchased by an investor over a decade ago and never developed. It had stayed desolate, save for the neighborhood kids who used it to ride dirt bikes on. I looked to my left, where the backs of the houses were. I hadn't even gotten a mile away from my house, which meant I could walk back and call my friend Samson, who happened to be the nicer of the two Hawthorne boys. Even if I walked in the other direction and reached the main road, it wasn't as if I couldn't wave someone down and ask them to take me to my destination. I reached for my phone just as the truck gave one last *tut* and rocked to a complete stop. I let out a grave sigh, looked at the completely empty service bar on my phone, and leaned my forehead against the top of the steering wheel.

This was the *last* shipment of fabric. It wasn't as if Hawthorne Industries needed it, but when Samson and I found it while he helped me clean out the garage, I told him I'd clean them up for him and deliver them. Having these in their possession wasn't a necessity on their end as much as it was on mine. I wanted to give it to them because it was another door closed, another part of what had become a cleansing ritual complete. I couldn't even remember why I'd signed up for the task instead of having Samson pick them up himself.

Probably because you're always trying to bite off more than you can chew. Probably because you're trying to overcompensate for the fancy school and the fancy degree. Probably because you truly are afraid to say goodbye to all of this and start a real, adult life.

I groaned loudly. Fuck my thoughts. Taking one last breath, I lifted my head and stepped out of the truck, walked to the front, and popped the hood. A cloud of smoke assaulted me, forcing me to retreat a step as I choked on my own exhale and waved the fumes away from my face.

"Need help?"

I jumped at the sound of the voice. Not *the* voice. *His* voice. Hard and gravelly and still the sexiest voice I'd ever heard. I clenched my fists, my nails digging into my flesh as I braced myself to turn around.

Don't snap. He's being nice, Tessa. Don't snap at him.

But the moment I turned around and my eyes met his, I snapped anyway.

"No, I don't need help. Especially not from you."

If he was upset, he didn't let it show. He sauntered over, ignoring me, and peeked under the hood of the truck. I crossed my arms and looked away so he wouldn't think I was checking out those muscular arms of his or that long, toned back that drove me wild (I was a back girl).

"Your engine is toast."

"I know that." I gritted my teeth. "You think I don't know that?"

"You want a ride?" He stood to his full six-foot-three stature and turned to me.

I lifted my chin and glanced away. *When pigs fly*, I wanted to say, but it sounded as childish as I felt around him, so I merely shook my head in response. I'd call Sam and tell him what happened. He'd gladly pick them up to appease me.

"Why are you delivering that, anyway?"

"I was cleaning out the garage and found it."

"I'm sure no one will mind if you keep it."

"I would." I narrowed my eyes at him. "I don't want to touch even a portion of what's no longer rightfully mine."

"Okay." He drew out the word with a slight frown. "Let me help you out then."

"I don't want or need your help." I waited for him to walk away, but he merely shook his head, glancing away to hide whatever emotion he felt, if he felt any at all. Stupid, emotionless man. "I'll figure it out."

"You're on a road that's only used by kids on dirt bikes, and it isn't even ten in the morning, there will be no dirt bikers until at least five. What are you going to do? Stand here until someone who isn't me comes along?"

"That would be ideal."

He muttered something under his breath and ran a hand through his hair. "You're being unreasonable."

"Oh. I'm sorry. I didn't realize I was. Hold on, let me change my façade into something better suited for you. What would you like? Happy-go-lucky Tessa? Smiling-but-doesn't-mean-it Tessa? Oh, I know, maybe the fall-all-over-you-brainless Tessa?"

His lips didn't move, but amusement lit in his eyes. I waited for him to say something cutting. Waited for him to call me a bitch or tell me to fuck off and jog his ass out of my sight. But he just stood there, watching me as if I were some kind of artwork in a museum that he couldn't figure out.

"I just want regular, always-has-a-comeback-for-everything Tessa to let me help her just this once."

I tore my gaze from his and looked back at my truck, thought about the stupid cleansing, goodbye ritual I was trying to accomplish. I should've added him to the back of the truck while I was at it. His mere presence was throwing me off. I looked at Rowan again.

"Fine. I guess I could use your help just this once."

He grinned and made his way to the bed of the truck. I

rushed over to make sure he didn't pick up the fabrics without the protector. The last thing I needed was his sweat all over them. I said this aloud, and he laughed, a deep chuckle I felt all the way down to my toes.

"You love busting my balls, don't you?"

"I wasn't aware you still had balls to bust."

He didn't laugh, but I saw the way his lips moved slightly just before he looked away. "You only have four rolls here. I can carry them, but it'll be easier if I go get my car instead. You know, so I won't mess any of them up with my human sweat," he said. "Do you want to come with me?"

"I can wait here."

I watched him walk in the direction of the houses and wondered if his car was at his parents'. My question was answered by how quickly he came back, his black car roaring as it came into view and stopped beside the beat-up truck. He got out, transferred the rolls from the bed of my truck to his backseat, and shut the door before wiping sweat off his forehead with the back of his arm.

"Is it okay if I go back and get a clean T-shirt?" he asked.

I clamped my jaw together to make sure my expression remained stoic. The last thing I needed was for him to notice the way my eyes fell over his tight, sweaty T-shirt.

"That's fine," I bit out as I slid into his passenger's seat at the same time as he slid into the driver's. "Though I don't understand why you didn't grab one while you were there."

"And deal with your wrath if I kept you waiting any longer? I value my life, thank you."

I tried and failed to bite back a smile.

"Why are you still driving that beat-up truck anyway?" he asked.

"What else would I drive?"

"I don't know. Any other car parked in the garage."

"There aren't any." I folded my arms across my chest.

"Hm. Must be nice to have a full house."

"Says the guy staying at his parents' house."

"There's no one at my parent's house except for me." He raised an eyebrow. "My brother is moving from his apartment to a bigger house, so he's been going by there to pick up the last of his things, but that's about it. I've barely seen him."

I frowned. "So why are you staying there?" And where were his parents living? I didn't want to ask this, of course, but I was dying to know.

"I'm waiting for construction on my apartment building to be complete. It should be move-in ready by October."

"Hm."

All sorts of questions popped into my head, but I pushed them aside. They'd go unasked because I didn't want to answer any more of his. Thankfully, he clicked for the iron gates that guarded his house to open and drove in, not pushing for an answer. My eyes stayed glued on those gates as we drove past them. They were like something out of a Richie-Rich movie, those gates, black with a gold emblem in the center. I'd seen them countless times, pushed them open in the middle of the night more times than I could count. I tore my eyes away and looked up at the house. I hadn't expected to feel such gripping emotion over a damn gate, but I guess some things never stop piercing your heart, no matter how much time passed.

"I'll be right out."

I nodded once and leaned against the seat before he jogged inside. I closed my eyes, trying to figure out how my trip had gone from closing a chapter in my life to being stuck in the middle of my epilogue. When Grandma Joan called me with a guilt trip, telling me to come spend a couple of weeks with her, I'd taken her up on the offer for two reasons: I was the only one left who hadn't packed her room and taken the boxes to the storage unit, and I missed her and this place. I missed the days I used to come here and feel like I was home. I missed the slow pace that came with a life here in Ithaca, nestled inside the city, but surrounded by nature and the water.

Thinking about those days also brought memories of Rowan. Kissing Rowan, holding hands with him, laughing with him in our canoes, but with the positive came the negative. He and I were never meant to be more than friends, and even friends was questionable. Friends didn't lie or omit important things. My eyes popped open when I heard the front door shut. I watched him take the steps two at a time and stride toward me.

He slid into the driver's seat, dropped one of the two bottles of water he'd been carrying into my lap, and shot me a wink. I scowled, clutching the water and facing forward. Just because I'd taken him up on the ride didn't mean we were suddenly going to be chums again. Far from it. I wouldn't fall for those mischievous eyes. I wouldn't fall for the panty-dropping grin either. I wouldn't fall. Not again.

CHAPTER TWO

ROWAN

"STOP SMILING." She scowled and glanced away.

I couldn't help it. I chuckled, though it was cut short by another one of her icy glares. Sliding out of my car, I realized she had no idea how much that little glare of hers turned me on. Most of the time, I wasn't sure which I preferred, the glare or the smile. I'd always dabbled in both when I had her. *Had* being the operative word there. I needed to remember that if this drive was going to go smoothly and I wanted any shot at seeing her again. Tessa's the kind of woman you couldn't jump to conclusions with. Years of platonic friendship taught me that.

We'd remained friendly enough after we ended things, especially before she left for college. I'd left a full year ahead of her and had come back for visits. We didn't always catch up—sometimes she'd be away with her family or friends while I was in town and I wouldn't see her. I hated those vacations. I started coming home less and less because of them. Home and Tessa were a package deal for me and on the occasions that she was absent, home seemed dull and uninviting. We called each other on birthdays, texted during holidays. Then, out of the blue, all of it stopped. I would've said it was just the way of life, people grow apart, but it wasn't a coincidence that she started pretending we were complete strangers after my parents bought her family's fabric company.

The handful of times I'd seen her after, she'd ignored me when I looked at her. If I walked into the same room, she'd pretend I wasn't there. When I had managed to get her to talk to me, she hadn't even looked me in the eyes. The only time she actually managed to meet my gaze was when she was glaring at me, which was ninety-nine percent of the time. None of that mattered. She was sitting with her back ramrod straight, her face tilted up slightly as she looked straight ahead. She had always been so beautiful. Beautiful, caring, and hardworking. With a heart of gold and a body that made a man think sinful, dirty thoughts. I swallowed those thoughts and started driving.

"When did you get back in town?" I'd been jogging by her house ever since I overheard my brother talking to her on the phone. I hadn't asked about it. I just pretended I wasn't listening as I followed him to the break room just to catch any information about her that I could. Unfortunately for me, I'd only managed to catch one laugh and one statement from him. And then I started jogging. As if I'd ever made jogging part of my workout in the past.

She glanced over briefly. "A couple of weeks ago."

"How long will you be here this time?"

She gnawed on her bottom lip, looking at the road ahead. "A few weeks."

"Hm. Leaving for good this time?" I was only half-joking. It was the one thing I'd clearly overheard my brother say on the phone.

"Actually, yes. For good this time."

I smiled. Tessa was one of those girls who wanted to get out of her town in a blink but would come back and visit so often you'd never know she'd been gone at all. She loved her parents and siblings too much to just ghost.

"Do you still want to design dresses?"

"Maybe." She shrugged.

"Where will you go?" I asked. "Did you get a job offer?"

Her face whipped in my direction. She had this wild look in those almond-shaped eyes of hers, as if she was unsure of what to do with everything I was asking. My chest squeezed as I waited.

"Why are you driving so slow? We should be there by now."

She was right. I was driving slower than I'd ever driven before, trying to savor the little time I had her in my presence.

"You didn't answer my questions."

"Yeah, on purpose."

Her words cut, but I didn't let it show. *I don't bleed.* It was something Dad drilled into us from a young age. Yes, people were all the same, we were all born and we would all die. The only thing really setting us apart was the way we chose to spend the short time we were alive. The difference between the Hawthorne's and everyone else was that in times of trouble, we were to remain stoic. It was what was expected of us, after all. I hadn't yet mastered my dad's uncaring characteristics or the way mom upturned her nose to everything she didn't approve of. Not sure if I ever would. As far as I knew, neither had my brother. I cleared my throat and turned my attention to Tessa. Kind, sweet, drop-dead-gorgeous-and-doesn't-know-it Tessa.

"I just want to know how you're doing."

"I'm doing well. I'll be better once I don't have to see you running down my block every morning."

A smile crept onto my lips. "I didn't think you noticed. You never look."

"You don't need one more woman looking at you."

"You're right. I only need one woman looking at me."

"Oh." She stayed quiet for a beat, and I thought I finally had her, but then she lifted her fiery gaze to mine and added, "Did Camryn finally move here?"

Fucking Camryn. The jab bothered me more than it should have. Tessa had every right to throw that in my face, and with the rumblings that were happening in regard to Hawthorne Industries, I wouldn't be surprised if Camryn took her claws out of the hedge fund manager she'd been fucking in New York and came back around to try to stake her claim on my last name again. It was what I would do if I were her. That was the thing about Camryn. Underneath everything, I saw pieces of myself in her loneliness. She wasn't like Tessa. Not the Tessa I knew, anyway.

I didn't feel like I knew this version of her. This mean, snappy woman who looked at me as if I were mud beneath her feet. Though, I had to admit, I did like the idea that she was a little jealous. Maybe I had a chance to right this after all.

She's leaving soon.

The thought crashed through me like a ten-foot wave. It was the same wave that crashed through me when I was set to leave for college and had broken things off with her because I didn't want her to think this had any chance of turning into a long-distance relationship. Later, I'd changed my mind about it and she'd waved the idea away. That was when the possibility that she'd never actually be mine hit me, and I selfishly started to hate myself for breaking things off to begin with.

After pulling into the parking lot much sooner than I would have liked, I threw the car into park and went to climb out, but she put her hand on my arm.

"It's okay. You don't have to help."

I willed my heart not to pound the way it was. *I do not bleed.* Damn it. "Sam's waiting for me. He'll help me get this stuff inside and take me home when I'm done. I'm sure you're dying to shower."

Her cheeks flamed when she said that, and she looked away to open the door. I would've reveled in it, but my jaw clenched at the mention of my brother's name. Before I had time to say anything smart, he was jogging outside, smiling at her as if she were the only person in the universe. My hands gripped the steering wheel. My brother was a good guy, the kind of guy you want your daughter taking home—hardworking and caring.

I considered myself a good guy, but I was selfish where he wasn't. I was driven where he was just okay with the position he'd been working in for years. He didn't even take Dad up on the offer of moving up in the company. I watched as Tessa got out of the car and wrapped her arms around him in a hug. Was it a friendly hug? Was it more than that? In spite of everything I'd once shared with my brother, in that moment, I hated him.

I knew I held no claim on her, but I hated Samson for having any part of her. Even when we were all just friends, they had understood each other on a level I hadn't quite been able to reach. It still bothered me. I would have killed to have just one tiny sliver of her affection still. Tessa did that to people. She was a light in this dark, ugly world, and with the power to turn your bad days around with a simple smile. *I let that slip away.* I agreed with that. I just didn't know why. I wanted to curse the day my parents bought her family's factory, but my self-importance wouldn't even let me do that. Regardless of that, I missed her.

"Hey, Ro. You coming inside?" Sam asked as he dipped into my back seat and gathered the fabrics.

"I'll be back in an hour."

Tessa opened the passenger door again and grabbed her bag. "Thanks for the ride," she said in a low, sweet voice I hadn't heard directed at me in ages. My eyes snapped to hers.

"I can go by and figure out what to do with the truck," I offered.

"No need. I'll have a tow truck go by there or have Sam go get it for me."

Sam. Fucking Sam. My own brother. "You getting cozy with my brother now?"

She shrugged as if to say they were together but not serious and then glanced away. I didn't like the way the burn of that shrug curled inside me, so I took a deep breath and let it out. I did not bleed. I shouldn't have even cared who she was with. Surely, she'd probably dated other guys in the last five years, but still, something about seeing it made it different. Maybe it was because it was my brother and dating each other's exes was supposed to be off the table.

"Well, thanks again." She pushed back and closed the door.

I lowered the window. "Tessa! Maybe we can have dinner sometime."

She pursed her lips. My heart raced. At least she was thinking about it. I felt a slow smile creep on my face and watched as she flushed.

"I'm not sure your girlfriend would appreciate that."

"Well, it's a good thing I'm single then."

She looked at me for a moment longer, chewing her bottom lip as she mulled over whatever it was she wanted to say. "I'll think about it."

I let out a breath and smiled. Thinking about it was better than flat out no.

CHAPTER THREE

TESSA

"DOES HE THINK WE'RE TOGETHER?" Sam asked as he drove me home.

"Who?"

He shot me an impatient look. I bit my lip and looked out the window to keep from answering. Maybe if he truly thought I didn't know whom he was talking about he'd leave me alone. It was highly unlikely, but a girl could hope. Sam rarely let questions go unanswered, and one look at my face would tell him I was full of it.

"My brother," he said. "He looked at me like he wanted to kill me."

"Who cares?" I shrugged.

"He's my brother."

"Doesn't he always look at you like that? I mean, you said yourself that you've barely spoken a word since he left for college." I raised an eyebrow. I didn't know the details, but I assumed they had a falling out. One of those absolutely absurd reasons that made no sense but made people lose touch completely. I guess I could have understood it if they weren't the only sibling the other had.

"I've been trying to fix things between us. Besides, even if I could dodge him at family functions, I'm going to have to put up with him at Hawthorne Fabrics for the rest of my life."

"It isn't like he's the boss there."

"Yet."

Yet. The word angrily made its way around my gut and festered. Rowan would fit into his father's shoes once he took over Hawthorne for good. He would also hate it if he knew I was comparing him to his father, not that it was an outlandish comparison when I considered the way he'd turned out. I turned my attention back to Sam.

"You never know, you may end up being the boss instead."

"I don't want to be the boss," he said. "I'm perfectly content with my brother having that role. He's business savvy, I'm not. He has the same drive that Dad has, I don't. I like the creative work, not the number crunching. I hate dealing with people, he loves it."

"I like that about you."

"I know." He smiled. "So? Does he think we're together?"

"I may have let him believe we might be together." I closed my eyes and cringed as I said the words. Sam chuckled.

"Why? You wanted to up the ante in our sibling rivalry?"

"I just didn't like the way he asked me if we were together, as if he deserves to be privy to any of that information, so I let him believe we were."

He stayed silent for a long moment before speaking. "You know, I've always thought mind games were dumb. Especially between two people who are clearly longing for each other."

"I don't long for him." I scoffed. "He's moved on. I've moved on. End of story."

He scoffed back. "You've moved on? With who? Me? Under false pretenses?"

"I dated guys in college," I said. "Besides, I don't need a man in order to say I've moved on. I've moved on with my life, period."

"Yet, you involve me in the mix because you know he'd have a problem with it. You knew he was jealous of our friendship even when you and he were together."

I rolled my eyes. "Well, that's bullshit because we're just friends. Besides, he has a girlfriend. I don't know why he cares about who I'm with."

"You know damn well Camryn isn't his girlfriend."

"Yet, we can't seem to place her in an alternative category."

"This isn't jeopardy, Tess," he said with an exhale. "Maybe it's force of habit. Or maybe he isn't over you."

"Let's go with the brother thing or even the force of habit. He and I weren't even together. Not really anyway."

"You were friends for a long time, though," he said.

"Yeah, and we should've stayed friends."

"Probably. Still, I find it hard to believe that two people as close as you two were can't salvage at least the friendship you had. It's sad, don't you think?"

"It is," I admitted.

It was the reason I regretted ever taking my relationship with Rowan to the next level. Even after we broke up, I didn't have it in me to hate him. I loved him too much for that. It hadn't been until the Hawthorne takeover happened that I started to hate him. He had known it was going to happen and hadn't thought to tell me. His father consulted everything with him. Everything. So there was no chance that he didn't know about it and he just didn't tell me anything. Not that my parents had said a word to me about it until it was done, but that was different. In their eyes, I'd forever be the baby of the family. They didn't need my approval to sell the company. Rowan used to call me for mindless things, but when something that important, that life changing, happened, I didn't get so much as a text. What was worse, when I sent him one, he left it unopened and unanswered.

The kicker was that my family's fabrics company wasn't the only one his parents bought. There had been four within a one-hundred-mile radius. Surely, they didn't need one more. They didn't need *ours*. If Rowan had told me, I would have come home and prevented it from happening. I could have convinced my dad not to sell. I would've done anything to keep Monte Industries out of it, including dropping out of the fancy ivy league school I was in and opting for a smaller college. It's not like Monte Industries was anywhere near as big as Hawthorne Industries, but the upholstery we made was beautiful and sought-out by all the local furniture companies. When I was little, I'd go to work with my parents and marvel that all of those people worked for us, making things my father had designed. Now, they all worked for the Hawthornes.

"You can't blame him for something he didn't have a say in," Sam said. "Trust me, I didn't even know about it."

"I can assure you he did, and I only blame him for not confiding in me. That sale ruined my family."

He shot me a sympathetic look. "I'm sorry."

"It isn't your fault."

"If you don't blame me, you shouldn't blame him either."

"Why are you so hell-bent on defending him today?"

He pulled into my driveway and then turned to face me. "Look, I have a lot of issues with my brother, but I can't fault him for what happened to your family. And you shouldn't either. Maybe if you try being friends with him again, you would be able to see that."

I shook my head. "Some things are better left alone."

"And some things are worth chasing. Friendship is one of them."

"Not with people you feel this strongly about."

His stared at me for a moment, looking like he wanted to say something more, but he just shook his head and looked out the windshield.

I sighed and reached for my door handle. "Thanks for the ride."

"I'll drive by the area where you said the truck died and call a tow truck to come get it."

"I can do that."

"Today was the last day of you bringing fabrics for me to lug in. Consider it a parting gift."

I smiled. "Thanks, Sam. You really are the better of the Hawthorne boys."

"Feel free to print that in the newspaper." He winked as he drove off, and I laughed as I headed inside.

CHAPTER FOUR

ROWAN

TESSA HAD CRAWLED into my head and made a little nest there long ago. In college, during those early morning bus rides with my teammates, I'd shut my eyes and pretend I was back in her truck. That led to thinking about her more than I should have. Normally, I could swat it away and ignore its existence, but this time, she seemed to be the only thing I could think about. Maybe it was because today was the first time in forever that I'd gotten to actually talk to her, but the only thing I seemed to be able to think about was the next time I could see her. If she didn't accept my dinner invitation, I wasn't even sure how I would see her again, short of me showing up at her house, but if that was what it took, I'd do it. That was the thing about Tessa. Once I caught a whiff of her, I seemed to crave her beyond comprehension. To this day, I couldn't explain it.

I sighed as I walked into the little restaurant I was set to have lunch with my mother in, which was not something I was looking forward to. Ever since my parents announced their split to us back in the spring, it had felt as if the world had turned upside down and I was left clinging on to anything that could withstand the storm brewing. Sam didn't know how good he had it, sitting back on the sidelines and getting to follow his creative passions. The whole giving-no-fucks vibe definitely had him at an even steeper advantage.

I spotted her dark brown hair almost immediately. Mom always had the same hairstyle—a sophisticated bun that kept the hair from her face. I cursed when I noticed the blonde sitting beside her and then wished I had been paying closer attention. Had I noticed sooner, I would have turned around and walked right out. I took a breath and kept my anger in check.

Camryn was always weaseling her way into my life. It wasn't enough that our parents were lifelong friends and we'd spent the majority of our childhoods and teen years in the same social circle. Nope, she had heard the rumors of my parent's divorce and how I was next in line to head the company, pulled her claws out of the Wall Street guy she was fucking in New York, and showed up here. It wasn't by chance. Nothing she did was. I knew it as surly as I knew my mother was happy about it.

Camryn smiled brighter when I came forward. "You look dashing today."

I ignored her compliment and kissed my mother on both cheeks before leaning in to do the same to her. Before I could pull away, she caught my jaw and gave me a peck on the lips. Mom raised her eyebrows as if to say, *something you want to tell me?* I shook my head and fought not to roll my eyes. She always got that look when Camryn was around, her barely masked approval was enough to make me uncomfortable.

I glared at my mother, who stifled a smile behind her mimosa.

Truth be told, Camryn and my mom weren't that different. I glanced at Camryn.

"What are you doing here?"

"Oh, I had a long layover on my way to San Fran and decided to make a day of it. I tried calling you, but it was going straight to voicemail. I figured you didn't have any reception out here in the country." I rolled my eyes. We were hardly in the country. "Anyway, I had lunch with a few friends and ran into your mom on my way out. Of course, I had to sit and keep her company while she waited for you."

"Well, I'm here now." Her smile dropped.

"I guess I'll leave you to discuss your private matters." She gathered her purse slowly, probably waiting to see if we were going to invite her to stay. Neither of us said a word as she stood and plastered another fake smile on her face. "Well, it was great chatting with you Mildred. I have a flight to catch."

"Always a pleasure, Camryn. Have a safe flight. Say hello to your mother."

"Of course. I'm sure she'll want to get together with you when you're in Paris next month. She's been missing everyone since moving away last year. I'll set something up, and maybe we can all grab dinner together." She smiled at me as she said it. I tore my gaze from her green eyes and looked at Mom.

"Sure, dear."

When she walked away, I felt the lead weight drop off my shoulders.

"She's dying for you to give her a chance."

"A chance to do what exactly? She manhandles me every opportunity she gets."

"And you let her."

"It's harmless." I shrugged. Sure, she'd caused trouble in the past, but that was then. I wasn't tied down to anybody now and the moment it came to that I knew how to deal with her.

"Sweetheart." Mom placed her hand over mine, beckoning me to meet her gaze. I did. "Women are never harmless. The faster you learn that, the better off you'll be."

I swallowed a mouthful of the mimosa the waiter just served me and tried to wash away the uneasiness her words brought. Mom had ordered a pitcher, and from the looks of it, she was either halfway to an afternoon nap or ready to party.

"I've never given her reason to believe I'd ever be interested in getting serious." I picked up the menu even though I knew I'd order my go-to steak and potatoes.

"Only serious enough to spend the night in her bed." Mom raised an eyebrow.

"I never spend the night in anyone's bed." It was the truth. Camryn and I had hooked up in high school and then again once in college, but it never went beyond that.

Mom rolled her eyes and took a long sip of her mimosa. "That's what your dad said about his mistress, and look at how that turned out. I ordered your usual for you, by the way."

I put the menu down and met her pained blue eyes. "You can't compare Dad's . . . affair to this."

"You're right. I'm sorry." She dabbed at her eyes with her napkin.

It was so weird to see my mom cry. She'd always shown so little emotion while we were growing up. The news of Dad's long-running affair with his secretary, a woman who had come to our house almost every day, had gone on family trips with us growing up, and had stopped by on holidays seemed to rip my mom open. Suddenly, she was crying and talking about feelings and asking about ours. I felt awful for her, but the selfish side of me liked this more emotionally available version of her. I just wish it'd come sooner, before her aloofness and Dad's absence and their combined loveless marriage scarred me irrevocably.

"Your brother still isn't answering my phone calls," she said. "Is he okay?"

My jaw clenched as I thought about Tessa with Sam.

"Why do you have that look on your face?" Her question made me blink out of my red haze.

"Sam's dating Tessa now. Maybe you should ask her how he's doing."

"Oh." Mom raised her eyebrows slightly. "They're good together." I shot her a glare. She shrugged. "She isn't good for you, Rowan. She never was. She's too young and naïve. You don't need a girl like that in your life."

"She's a woman now, Mom."

"Just as well. Anyhow, I was hoping to speak to both of you together before my trip," she said. "Your father and I are keeping this divorce private until everything is finalized with the company, but I wanted to fill you in on the basics. We're talking about splitting Hawthorne Fabrics down the middle."

My eyes widened. "What? What is there to split? Won't that cause friction with the accounts we currently have?"

"It'll be a quiet split," she said, shooting me an irritated look. Mom hated interruptions. "It'll be divided between the States and Europe accounts."

"What about South America? Asia?" That earned me another look.

"I'm getting to that, Rowan." I swallowed and sat back. Waited. My knee started to bounce underneath the table. "Asia and South America will also be split between both companies. We're bidding for those."

"Bidding? You're going to get into a bidding war?" Unbelievable. She blinked prettily, the way she often did in front of my father in order to get her way. I ignored it. "Do we have a say in this?"

"No. Your father and I will discuss it and get back to you. I just want you to understand what's happening."

I pushed out a deep breath, shook my head, and dug into the steak and potatoes the waiter placed in front of me. A part of me hoped she'd say that my brother and I would have to hash it out, leave the decision to us. Maybe if we were forced to work together, we could salvage the friendship we once had, the one where we put each other over everything and everyone.

When Mom spoke again, it was about family, about marriage and kids, and about building something of my own. I'd heard the story a million times, but listening to it right then made a sick feeling twist in my stomach. My grandparents had opened the textiles company in the basement of their two-bedroom town-house. The moment my parents were married, they became a project to my grandparents. A way to expand the brand. Eventually, they let Dad run the company and while he'd made good business decisions. He decided to buy out Monte Industries, something I would've done given the chance. If Tessa's father had been business-minded and hadn't thought of Monte as more of a passion project, they'd be the ones owning us and not the other way around. They'd had the factories and labor workers, the room to grow. They just didn't act on it. Mr. Monte was always too focused on the creative aspect of the company, not the business side of things.

The only place I could see that Dad went wrong was not buying out the company from my grandparents. Whether it be because the growth wasn't as fast as he'd originally intended or he didn't want to do that to his old man, I'd never know. It would be one of the first things I would do if I ever had a chance though. Sam didn't care about our inheritance or his role in the company. Whereas, I'd been primed for this from age seven when Dad started taking me to work with him every summer. Sam would go sometimes, but he wasn't required to the way I was. When he did go, it was for an allowance.

We weren't the spoiled rich guys outsiders may have thought we were. We'd been raised to work for our money. We had allowances growing up, had worked for our first cars, and had paid for our own car insurance. Even though we lived in a nice house and went to top-notch schools, we hadn't been spoiled the way a lot of our friends had been. Nowadays, I was grateful for that. I was also grateful for the work ethic my father had instilled in me. It was probably the one thing I could say I learned from him.

"I know your hearts aren't in this—"

"Samson's heart isn't in it, but mine is. Otherwise, why would I even entertain this conversation?"

"Contracts are important to abide by," she said. "Marriage being one of them."

I blinked. I knew where marriage fit into Hawthorne. I just hadn't put much thought into it in regard to myself and the company. As far as I was concerned, marriage was a business transaction. On occasion, when Tessa's limbs were wrapped around mine, I'd had fleeting thoughts about marriage, but I ended our relationship before any of that could be a serious notion. Even if I hadn't, even if I genuinely believed in the sanctity of those vows, my parents' divorce would have changed that. Love was an illusion. An idea that society tried to sell to you. I believed in respect and honesty, but love? Love had never been on my radar.

CHAPTER FIVE

ROWAN

Past

DAD ALWAYS WOKE me up at seven o'clock on Saturday mornings. It was the day we went around and visited our customers. Samson came along sometimes, but not usually. He wasn't expected to. He had baseball games on Saturdays that Grandpa Pete took him to, games that dad made me stop playing because he needed me to be his sidekick. I'd called myself a side-kick to help me get through the boring days, but really, I was more like an accessory. Even my thirteen-year-old-self knew that.

By the time we pulled up to Monte Industries, it was ten in the morning. We'd already gone to three other manufacturing companies before this stop. All three had been the same, husband talking shop with Dad while I sat there silently pretending to pay attention and the wife offered me cookies and milk and finally a juice box. By the time we pulled up at Monte Industries, I'd had three juice boxes and thought if I saw one more cookie I'd puke. I wasn't much of a sweets kid.

Mr. Monte smiled as he said hi to Dad and smiled wider when he saw me in tow.

"Little working man," he'd said. "I need to put Freddie to work on Saturday mornings."

"You gotta start them young," Dad said with a gleam in his eyes that made me warm inside. Maybe he was proud of me after all. I mean, I did come along while all the other kids my age were obviously sleeping or doing fun things.

"I heard you're going to start rowing for the school team soon," Mr. Monte said. "Will you still have time to come by on Saturdays?"

"He'll have to make up his work whenever he's free," Dad answered, patting my head. "He's next in line to take over the company so he needs to learn the ropes."

We walked inside and sat in Mr. Monte's upstairs office, which overlooked the employees downstairs. After ten minutes of listening to them talk about my mom and Mrs. Monte and how important family was in all of this, I tuned them out and looked out the window. Everybody was either sewing, stapling or rolling fabric rolls in plastic to keep it safe. The door opened suddenly and a few people stopped to wave at Tessa, who walked in wearing her ballet outfit – pink tights and a pink leotard. She wore converse sneakers on her feet, but was holding a pink bag that I knew held her pointe shoes. I looked over my shoulder.

"May I use the restroom?"

"Of course," Mr. Monte said. Dad shot me a warning look that made me shiver, but I walked out of the office nonetheless. Dad hated when I interrupted conversations or asked for anything, including the restroom. I ran downstairs and scanned the room for Tessa. I found her sitting in front of the coffee machine in the break room. Her head snapped up when I walked into the room. My heart beat a little faster.

"Working again?" she asked.

"Yeah." I exhaled and sat in the chair across from her. "So boring."

"Why doesn't Sam do it?"

"Because he's not expected to. He's the baby of the family, not the first born."

"Hm." She gave me a sad, but understanding smile, probably because she herself was the baby of her family. "At least you know what you're going to be when you grow up."

"Don't you?" I waved a hand around.

"Yeah. Well, I mean, I hope. I'm not the first born." Her eyes twinkled when she said that. She was the prettiest girl, especially when she smiled like that. "What would you be when you grow up, if you could be anything?"

I shrugged. "The president of Hawthorne Industries."

"That's it?" She laughed. "That's what you're going to do anyway. I mean if you didn't have to do that."

"Same answer."

Her eyes searched mine for a long moment, as if she were waiting for me to change my mind. Tessa's parents encouraged growth and being whatever you wanted to be. I'd been waking up early on Saturdays since I was five years old. Hawthorne Industries was the only thing I knew and the only thing I was expected to do with my life. I fully accepted it. Tessa kept talking about her day. She was dropped off here after ballet because she wanted her dad to take her to the mall to buy presents for her brother and sister. After listening to her for a while, I said goodbye went back upstairs, knowing that if I was gone too long there would be hell to pay later.

In the car, Dad reprimanded me for taking too long in the bathroom. "It's not responsible. You need to learn the difference between work and fun."

"I do know the difference. That's why I'm not hanging out with my friends and I'm here instead."

That earned me a hard look and a pop on the mouth. "You don't bleed," he said. "Remember that. You're not like those other kids. You have things to do with your time and your life."

I held my hand to my lips. He said I couldn't bleed, but the thick liquid in my mouth said otherwise. I held back the hot, frustrated tears that threatened to spill out of my eyes, knowing that would only earn me more than just a pop in the mouth. Crying was a sign of weakness. I'd learned that from watching Mom trying to buy his affection through tears. The only thing it did was ensue a screaming fit from him that included name calling and belittling. Just the other night during dinner, Sam brought up a bad grade, and Dad yelled and told him he was stupid and stupidity didn't belong in this family. I'd held my brother's hand under the table to let him know I was with him no matter what, but I didn't stand up for him. That was three nights ago and I was still kicking myself for not standing up to my father. He made it difficult, though. He was quick to remind us how insignificant we were and I didn't want that reminder. Not when I felt it every night when I was in my room trying to find sleep and my parents screamed about what a mistake we were.

CHAPTER SIX

TESSA

I CLOSED my eyes and inhaled the scent of pine that surrounded me. It may have reminded the rest of the world of Christmas, but for me, it was the smell of home. I opened my eyes and let out a deep, cleansing breath before continuing toward the red canoe. I pushed it away from the dock and climbed in just as the tip glided into the water, picking up the paddle and making my way to my favorite relaxing spot. I went slowly, enjoying the way the paddle felt as it sliced through the still water. When I finally reached the little bank in the middle of the lake, I pulled the paddle in, made sure it was secure, and laid back to let my muscles relax.

I used to go much farther than this without complaints from my shoulders, which told me I was definitely not in shape like I used to be. It didn't help that I paddled by myself. Usually, Freddie or Celia helped. Then again, usually, canoes and jet skis filled the lake, and out farther, sailboats dotted against the skyline. I guess that was what happened when everyone in the neighborhood grew up together. They got older and started their lives and left at the same time.

I kept my eyes closed and tried to force my brain to think about something else, something positive, but it was no use. Being back only brought on old memories. Not that they were all bad. I'd had a pretty damn good home life before Dad decided to sell to Hawthorne. Still, I had great friends, most of who had graduated college and gone onto grad school or were getting married. Even my memories of Rowan made me smile most days. I thought about what Sam said to me yesterday. Maybe I could be friends with him again, who knows? My canoe rocked lightly, and my eyes popped open. I gripped both sides and sat up quickly, twisting to see who was out here. It could be the people in charge of cleaning up the water, though, judging from how clean it was, I'd bet money they had already done it. I brought my hand up to shield the sun from my face and squinted in the direction of a bright blue canoe. My heart sped up.

From where I sat, I couldn't tell if it was Sam or Rowan, but I would know that canoe anywhere. Unlike mine, theirs was a professional vessel. A single scull, Rowan had once told me. That was the official term for it. The kind they used in the Olympics. The kind that took me more than a handful of tries to get a handle on but Rowan maneuvered as if it were his own skin. He called it Miles. Miles was blue and shiny and made you not want to look away from it once it rowed past you, much like his owner.

Rowan had been on the crew team in high school and college. I'd woken up more than enough times at four a.m. and accompanied him to tournaments. Heck, even after we'd gone our separate ways, I'd heard that he'd gotten Columbia more than a few trophies as captain. I wasn't surprised one bit.

As he got closer, I settled into a more comfortable position and willed my heart to stop acting like a rabbit being chased. The single scull kissed the side of my nameless wooden canoe as Rowan expertly situated himself beside me. I made myself look at him, and my breath caught. He'd always been gorgeous, but damn. I wasn't sure many people could top Rowan. I dated a football player in college, but even he paled in comparison. Maybe it was because, for some crazy reason and despite myself and what I wanted, I felt connected to Rowan on a deeper level.

"It's quiet out here," he said.

I glanced away from his tempting, bare chest and focusing on the seemingly endless water before us. "It was."

"You trying to kick me out, Sprite?"

My heart did a little dip. I'd hated that nickname when I was young. I'd always thought it was a way to make fun of me and my small, slightly pointy ears, but hearing it stirred up something deep inside me.

Don't fall for it, Tess. Don't you dare fall for it.

"Even I know I don't have the power to kick Poseidon out of the water."

He chuckled, and I leaned back in my canoe, closing my eyes once again. The soft scuff of fabric against wood told me he was doing the same. "I'm not used to this being so empty in the summer."

"Everyone's gone."

"Why do you think that is? We all grew up here. Have had a pretty good life. Why did we all leave?"

I sat up. "I don't know. Why'd you leave?"

"School." He frowned as if he wanted to add something. I would've bet money it was to get away from his family, the way most of us wanted to do during that time.

"Most of us left for the same reason."

"But not everyone is willing to come back."

"Are you coming back?"

"I'm already back. I would've been back sooner, but I wanted to finish my master's degree before coming back." He watched me closely. "Are you?"

"I have nothing to come back for." I turned away and faced the sun again, adjusting my bikini top as I did.

"What about your family? You've always been tight-knit."

I scoffed, wondering if all the time he'd spent outdoors rowing had messed up his brain. Surely, he knew my family was completely and utterly broken. Even if he hadn't heard it from Sam, this was a small enough community for him to have heard the rumors. Hell, I couldn't walk down the street without hearing whispers about it. Between that and the rumors about Camryn and Rowan getting cozy in college, I'd spent an entire year with my head down. What was worse was the way people talked about them, as if they knew they were destined to be together and were glad they'd finally figured it out. It made me want to scream, *"What am I? Chopped liver?"* I never would, of course, but the words were always on the tip of my tongue.

"How's your dad?" I asked, staying on topic. I didn't care whether his mother was doing well or not. As far as I was concerned, she was dead to me after the last conversation we'd had. He looked away, placing his elbows on either side of his canoe. I tried not to focus on the way every single muscle on his back and arms flexed with each motion.

"I'm sure you've heard from my brother."

"I want to hear it from you."

His attention whipped in my direction. "Why?"

"Because I want the real version, not the watered-down version that pretends the world is a beautiful place."

"I thought you liked that about Sam." His gaze held mine with intensity, like he knew something I wasn't telling him. It threatened to pull me under. To make me want to snatch all the lies back, put them in a bottle, and put a cork in it. I cleared my throat. He didn't deserve my truth. He hadn't earned that much from me yet.

"Tell me."

"Dad's fine, as usual. Mom, however, is an emotional mess," he said. My brows rose. He chuckled. "I know. I never thought I'd see the day. I think she's told me she loves me more in the last six months than she has my entire life."

My heart felt heavy at his admission. His parents had really done a number on him and Samson. Somehow, they'd settled on extreme ends of the social ladder, but the outcome was the same. They both felt like they were unloved, as if they weren't enough. I'd never understand how two people could have such beautiful children and let them grow up to feel that way.

"Dad has practically moved on with his new family, as if none of us existed. I meet with him in the mornings, but it's strictly work. I'm sure I'll see less of him when the division is complete."

My attention whipped to him, and I narrowed my eyes. "What division?"

"They're getting a divorce and splitting up Hawthorne Fabrics."

"What?" My heart climbed into my throat as I fought to digest the news. "After everything?"

"It was inevitable. They should have never merged their companies to begin with. All it did was create . . ." His voice drifted as he continued his rant.

My brain stayed stuck on the fact that they were splitting up

Hawthorne Fabrics. My hands gripped the paddle and, as if on autopilot, I started to row back to the shore. I could hear Rowan's voice behind me, but I couldn't make out his words. My father sold his company, everything he'd worked for, and they were splitting it up as if it were nothing to them. Because of a lousy divorce? It was stupid. The entire thing was stupid, and the Hawthorne's were cursed. I reached the dock and scrambled out of the canoe, tripping over my feet as I did so. Thankfully, I managed to stay upright and keep walking.

"Tessa!" Rowan shouted behind me. I kept moving. Maybe if I picked up my feet fast enough, I'd make it back without having to speak another word to him. I was leaving in two and a half weeks. Surely, I could avoid him until then. Surely, he wouldn't hound me everywhere I went. He gripped my arm and spun me around. I met his fiery gaze, eyes wide.

"What the hell? I was talking to you."

"I was done listening."

"Tough luck. You can't just walk away when you have a problem with reality."

I scoffed. "Look who's talking. The king of running away from things he's afraid of!"

"I don't run away." He stepped closer, looming over me, the heat of his skin kissing across my own. "And I'm not afraid of anything."

"You're afraid of everything!" I screamed, slapping a flat hand over his hard chest. "Everything."

"Bullshit. You're the one who's always afraid." He pushed his chest against my hand, which was still lingering on his chest, a stupid excuse of a barrier, especially when all I could think about was the way his warm, muscled chest felt beneath my touch. "You're afraid of leaving, afraid of staying behind, you're always stuck in a state of guilt for every decision you make because you're too fucking afraid to follow what your own heart wants."

I pursed my lips, ironically still stuck between storming away and keeping my hand right where it was.

"Tell me I'm wrong," he challenged. "Tell me you didn't pick the university I told you *not* to go to because you were afraid you'd follow me and we'd actually have a shot at something real."

"I did follow my heart! I went to my dream school. The school I'd wanted to go to long before you walked into my life." I brought my other hand up and pushed him hard. He didn't budge. He just pressed against both of my trembling hands. "And for the record, you wouldn't know real if it smacked you in the face. That was why you broke things off with me, and that was why you chose Camryn."

He growled, and in one swift motion, he grabbed me around the waist, dragged my body flush against his, and ducked his head. His mouth crushed against mine so hard and fast that I was forced to bring my hands up to his biceps and hold on. I'd kissed Rowan thousands of times, but this kiss was unlike any other. This kiss made the air swoosh out of my lungs. His tongue swept into my mouth and demanded I bend to its will, stroking mine with a precision that made Leonardo da Vinci's brush pale in comparison. He slid his fingers into my hair and massaged my scalp as he commanded the kiss. I heard myself moan, felt the liquid heat between my thighs, and gripped his muscled arms tighter. He pulled back slightly and teased my lips with light nips. It was then that my eyes popped open. I ripped my mouth from his and pushed him away.

"What the hell is wrong with you?" I shouted, panting. He stared at me with an odd expression on his face, as if he wasn't sure where he was standing or how he'd gotten there. When he didn't respond, I turned and sprinted away as fast as my wobbly legs and sandaled feet would allow.

CHAPTER SEVEN

TESSA

Past

"SO, you get that perfect tan from your grandmother, huh?" Rowan asked as he walked over to me.

I was standing in the wooded area of the lawn by the fire pit, which was where I normally hung out during parties like these. Tonight was my grandmother's birthday party and my siblings had gone out of town, something they'd planned before Mom planned this party, and while I definitely thought I'd be alone,

Rowan's presence made me giddy, though, it wasn't only because I didn't want to be bored and alone.

"I guess so. You've never seen her before?" I smiled as I answered his question, tucking my hair behind my ear. "I could've sworn you had."

"Never had the pleasure. She must travel a lot."

"She travels back and forth to France. My grandfather left her a Chateau."

"Is that why you were in France last summer?"

"Yeah." I nodded, hoping the darkness and my complexion were enough to hide my flush.

My heart hadn't managed to contain itself from the moment he walked through the door, and it didn't matter how much I told myself that it was because I'd been bored until he got here. The truth was that I'd sported a crush on him for quite some time. I could tell you virtually everything about him, from the specks of gray in his blue eyes to where he sat in the coxswain during rowing matches. Still, we were just friends. Just friends. He was more of Freddie's friend than mine. I constantly reminded myself of this whenever he walked by me in the halls and winked and my girlfriends squealed and freaked out. He was a year older than I, but I still managed to snag two AP classes that he was in. Thank God for small miracles like small private schools with limited AP. I was the only junior in a class with three seniors. Also the only junior in the school that would graduate ahead of my class and start college a semester ahead.

Normally, Rowan hung out with Freddie and Sam. Tonight, our siblings weren't around to buffer our interactions. Celia was away scouting colleges; Freddie had gone with her. Samson was on a trip with his girlfriend. That left Rowan and I alone in the woods, quite literally. I would have sworn he'd be at Emma Wesley's party, his rumored girlfriend, whom I wanted to hate so badly but was too nice to warrant those feelings from me. It was stupid for me to hate her at all. It wasn't like Rowan kept girls around. He was the kind of guy who had a new girlfriend or fuck-buddy or someone to keep him company every few weeks. Samson said he got bored quickly. I thought he hadn't met the right girl, and that included me. I wasn't naïve enough to think I'd be the one to tame the beast inside him. I hadn't even thought about trying.

I changed the subject. "I'm surprised you're here tonight."

"Where am I supposed to be?"

"Emma Wesley's party."

"Why would I be there?"

I settled back against the tree trunk behind me. "Aren't you two dating?"

"Define dating." I could hear the playful tone in his voice, but I wasn't having it. I lifted my chin and met his eyes.

"I'm not Freddie or one of your crew boys. Are you dating or not?"

"Not," he said, pausing before continuing. "She wanted to get serious, I didn't, so she broke it off. I heard she's dating Erick Gnash."

"The quarterback?"

He nodded.

"Well, she certainly has a type." Erick was one of the cutest kids in school. Even Celia had a crush on him, and she was a senior, in the same class as Freddie and Rowan. Perks of being born ten months after your older brother and having a birthday that coincided with state laws.

"She's a nice girl." A nice girl but not what he wanted, I supposed. I wondered if it was because what he wanted was tall, blonde, and obnoxious. I didn't bother pointing that out. If I did, he'd think I was interested, and I wasn't. Not at all.

Liar.

I whisked the little voice away with the shake of my head.

"How'd it go at your last meet?"

"We won. You should've come."

"You only want me to go because all of you fit in my truck."

After that, he was silent for the longest time before asking, "So, where is your grandmother from anyway?"

I had totally been staring at his profile, which was just about perfect. Long lashes, chiseled jaw, long nose, plump lips. His Adam's apple bobbed as he took another sip of his drink. Even his neck was nice. I blinked away from my thoughts and remembered he'd asked a question. Right. My grandmother.

"New Zealand."

"Hm." He looked at me for a moment. "Where is that?"

"Near Australia." I felt my lips pull up at the corners. People always had funny reactions to that. His brows scrunched together as he took a sip.

"Right," he said slowly, as if remembering the geography. "It's an island."

"Tiny island."

"With beautiful women," he said.

I felt myself blush, bit my lip, and glanced away. Was he calling me beautiful?

Maybe he's saying your grandmother is beautiful, moron.

Grandma Joan was quite stunning, after all, and he'd never cast me a second glance before. Why would he start? I clutched my own cup tighter when I heard him speak again.

"Do you know anything about it?"

"Like do I know how to speak Māori?"

"If that's the language." His lips twitched. I felt my face go hot at the mere sight of it.

"I know a few things but not much."

"Like what?"

I took a sip, my eyes set on his. He watched me expectantly. I mulled over the things my grandmother had taught me, which hadn't been much if I were being honest. She was barely one year old when her parents moved to the States. It wasn't as if she remembered anything about her birthplace, but her parents had made it a point to teach her about her roots, and she tried to do the same for my mother, which was where it stopped. Mom said she couldn't feel a connection to a place she'd never visited. I took a breath, leaned down to set my cup on the grass, and made my way over to him. The shade of his eyes became clearer with each step that I took. My heart shook, but I managed to close the distance between us and stood directly in front of him. He waited.

"*Tena koe* is how you say hello," I explained. "It means, 'I see you.'"

"*Tena koe,*" he repeated, his eyes set on mine.

If he'd ever looked at me like this before, I had never been aware of it, and I was glad for it because I felt like I was on a ledge with no place to go. Maybe it was the fact that we were alone. Maybe it was all of the changes happening in my life, with my siblings moving away soon. Whatever the reason was, it urged me to act on something I had wanted to do for as long as I could remember. I took a step closer, reached my right hand up and cupped the back of his neck. He lowered the hand holding his drink so there was nothing between us, and I pulled him closer to me. He didn't close his eyes the way I would have if I thought someone was about to kiss me. He also didn't back away the way I would have if I had a boyfriend and someone who wasn't him was about to kiss me. He simply looked at me, searching my eyes quickly, as if to make sure I wanted this. If my pulse hadn't been spiking the way it was, I would have laughed because, hell yes, I wanted to kiss him, but it wasn't what I was doing.

"This is called a *hongi,*" I whispered. "It's how they greet each other. You have to press your forehead against mine, your nose against mine, and breathe out."

"Why?" he whispered back.

"To indicate that we're all equal—one soul."

He took a step back. I dropped my hand from his neck. He looked at me warily, his eyes jumping between mine, searching for God only knows what. I waited. That was how things were with Rowan. He liked to process his thoughts and feelings while people waited. I knew his game, knew that if I pushed him, he'd freak out. So, I watched as the wheels turned in his head.

"Okay," he said after a few beats. "Let's try this again. This is how everyone greets each other? Man and man, woman and woman, woman and man?"

I nodded and felt myself smile. He ran a hand through his hair and exhaled a shaky laugh.

"My dad can't seem to hug us, yet people in New Zealand are doing this?"

My smile dropped. His parents were assholes. When we were kids, while his brother and the rest of us were in tee-ball and ballet, Rowan was spending his Saturdays in meetings with his father. They'd come by Monte Industries and I'd catch the bored, faraway expression on his face. He'd found rowing in our early teens and stuck with that every weekend since, and I got the impression that his boat, Miles, saved him in a way. My mind drifted back to his father and his refusal to show affection to his sons.

"You want to talk about it?"

"No." He frowned, looking away from me and back to the party, back to the adults who thought what they did was so much more important than raising responsible, caring individuals. He sighed and looked back at me. "What else do you know?"

"That's basically it."

His lips twitched. "So, we can't go on a trip to New Zealand any time soon?"

"Guess not."

"Hm." He stepped closer again, close enough that I could smell his Jean Paul cologne and feel the heat from his body. He brought his arm up, splaying his large hand on the side of my neck, his thumb rubbing my jaw gently. I wondered if he could feel the way my pulse skittered under his hold, wondered if he knew just how deep my feelings for him ran. If he did, he didn't let on. If he did, he'd run. I knew that much. The Hawthorne boys only gave you small particles of themselves, enough to make your cells lose balance while their own regenerated. He held my gaze steady as he dipped his head and placed his forehead against mine, his nose touching mine. Then he closed his eyes. I followed suit. And we breathed. He inched closer. I did the same. Without preamble, his lips touched mine. I jolted but managed to keep my eyes closed, mainly because if this were a dream, I wanted to remain sleeping, preferably forever if Rowan Hawthorne was going to continue to kiss me. I stifled a breath, a whimper, anything that would threaten to pull us out of this haze. I wondered if he knew how long I'd dreamed of this, if he had any idea that every time I looked at his lips, I imagined them on mine.

His fingers threaded into the hair on the nape of my neck as he pulled my head back slightly so he had a better angle against my mouth. His teeth nipped my bottom lip softly before he sucked it into his mouth with a groan that seemed to develop in the back of his throat. I shivered against him, brought both hands up to the back of his neck, and pulled him closer, feeling like the distance between us was too much.

He pushed me against the large tree trunk and slanted his mouth over mine once more. This time, the action was more desperate, his tongue sliding into my mouth in search of mine. I felt myself free fall into the kiss in a way that terrified me. I'd always wanted Rowan, but I had stayed away from him because a part of me knew that it would be like this—an intense push and pull that neither one of us was ready for. It was that thought that had me breaking the kiss and rearing away slightly. I kept my gaze on his chest, unwilling to meet his eyes just yet.

"I fucked this up, didn't I?" he said, his voice a rough whisper that did crazy things to me.

I began shaking my head, but he caught my chin and tilted my face up to look at him. His gaze was intense and hazy and did nothing to settle my thrumming heartbeat. He leaned in, pressed his lips to my forehead, and walked away without another word.

CHAPTER EIGHT

TESSA

HE OWED it to me to respect my privacy. That was what I told myself when I glanced up from my sketchbook and saw him walk into the coffee shop. I was tempted to slide out of the booth and leave, but I got here first. His eyes found mine quickly, as if he'd heard my thoughts from way over there. My heart skittered at the look he gave me, raw and heated as it stilled the breath in my lungs until he finally looked away and toward the girl behind the counter. Jenny, the barista, was already flirting with him. I wasn't even sure he realized it; his face was stoic. She was cute. Cuter than Camryn. Nicer than Camryn. If I had come home and found out he was dating a girl like her, it wouldn't have bothered me . . . much.

I looked at my sketchbook and sighed, ripping out the page and starting over. In my periphery, I tracked his approach. I kept my eyes on the sketchbook, trying not to react at the scent of his cologne. He'd worn my favorite one, and Rowan wasn't the kind of man who left things up to coincidences, so that alone made me think he knew he'd run into me today. He took the seat across from me and sat in silence, but I could feel his eyes on mine as I sketched.

Some people are shy about their art. I never understood that. My sister was like that. She hid her writing and poetry until she landed an agent. I didn't bother to hide my sketches. Art was something meant to be seen, to be read, to be felt. It didn't have to be great, it just had to carry emotion. Rowan picked up my discarded paper and examined it.

"What's wrong with this one?"

My hand paused on the sketch I was working on, but I didn't look up. "Wasn't feeling it."

"Why'd you rip it out of your notebook?"

I shrugged. "I don't like looking at my mistakes."

"You should learn from your mistakes."

I lifted my eyes to his. "I like to move past them."

"By ignoring them?" he said, lifting the to-go cup to his mouth. I swallowed as if I was the one taking a drink, shrugged again, and tore my eyes from his. Turning away was hard, but I did it, dropping my eyes to the sketch in front of me, the one I hadn't fucked up yet. I wasn't going to get into this argument in the middle of the coffee shop. This was my safe zone. He shouldn't be here.

"This is good, Tess. Really good."

My heart glowed with his praise. Stupid organ. "Thanks."

"I'm serious." His mouth was slightly parted, and his attention was still on the paper of the dress I was drawing when I dared to let my eyes find his again. "I'm impressed."

"I can tell." I laughed, felt myself blush. "Thank you."

"Is this your own design or are you practicing from someone else's?"

"My own."

His brows lifted. "Who'd you get an internship with?"

"Apprenticeship," I corrected. "And I never said I got one." I couldn't bite back my smile as I said the words. Rowan grinned that knowing grin of his that made my heart flutter. I tried to contain myself so it wouldn't affect me. It didn't work.

"Talent like this doesn't go unnoticed."

"Talent goes unnoticed all the time. People walk right by it at subway stations or hang it on their fridge and never give it a second glance. Talent is probably the second most overlooked thing in this world."

"What's the first?"

"Love."

Obviously, things like that weren't always apparent to him. He looked away, uncomfortable. The word alone made him so, which set off a slow-building and unwanted mix of sadness and anger inside me. The way he was raised did that to him, I got that, but what made me angry was that he hadn't snapped out of it. Sam was the same. They were both ridiculously good-looking men who had both money and power but didn't have a fucking clue how to accept something so many were willing to give so freely. He cleared his throat and looked at me again.

"So? Apprenticeship?"

"I was offered two. One in New York and one in Paris."

His brows hiked up. "Paris?"

"I know." I smiled sadly.

"You aren't going to take that one?" He leaned forward on his elbows. "Why do you keep doing that to yourself? Why do you keep flapping those incredible wings of yours like they've been clipped? Why won't you let yourself soar?"

Anger seared through me. How dare he appear out of the blue and decide he can make claims he doesn't know a thing about? I lifted my chin. "Why don't you mind your own business and go build your empire with your Stepford wife?"

"She isn't my wife, nor will she ever be."

"You always say things like that right before you run back to her."

He shot me a glare that made me want to cower. "What happened to you?"

"I don't know what you're talking about."

"You used to be . . . I don't know . . . cordial with me."

"I was going to try to be cordial with you again, but then you kissed me."

His smile was slow, wolfish. "You liked it."

I dropped the pencil, picked it back up, and continued shading. I wouldn't allow him to drag me down that place with him again, the one where we flirted and kissed and frolicked around town holding hands. Rowan was well versed in the art of having women fall in love with him and leaving them behind. I saw him do it time and time again. I wasn't sure why I ever thought I would be different.

"Why are you so upset?" he asked.

"Your parents convinced mine to sell them their company," I said quietly. "They knew it was all they had, and still they went after them until they couldn't say anything but yes. You Hawthorns don't know how to take no for an answer."

"That isn't true."

I cocked my head. "Really?"

"No one ever says no. There's a difference."

"Stop veering off topic. My point is that we sold our family business, the one thing we've had passed down from generation to generation. Then, once it was out of our hands, it ripped my parents apart."

"And, somehow, this is my fault?"

"You knew what was happening, and you didn't even think to warn me." He gave a nod, and took a sip of coffee as I continued on because the way he was looking at me pissed me off. "All you needed to do was pick up the phone and give me a heads-up. Unless you didn't know?"

"No," he said. I started to let out a relieved breath. If he didn't know there was no foul. "I knew. I just didn't want to tell you."

My chest squeezed. I gripped my pencil a little tighter. If it didn't snap, I wouldn't either. Solidarity and all that shit.

"Why didn't you tell me?"

"Because I knew you wouldn't approve."

"Obviously." I rolled my eyes for good measure and stared as I waited for him to continue. He had an amused look on his face, that little twinkle in his eyes that never let up. When he finally spoke, I found myself leaning in a little closer.

"My dad didn't go to yours about buying his company."

"He bought us all out." My voice lifted with my hand as I pointed outside. "He bought all the factories within a fifty-mile radius."

"He didn't want to buy yours. He knew how much it meant to you guys. Even if he had, Mom wouldn't have let him."

"Right." I scoffed. "Because they're so fucking caring."

"Maybe not with us," he said. "But they look after their friends. They respect your parents."

I thought about just how much his mother respected me. "Don't mind me, I'm just sitting here waiting for an explanation."

"Your parents sold to us so they could pay for your school. The business wasn't doing well. Dad tried to talk them out of it, and when he couldn't, he gave them more than it was worth."

His words shot through me like a tsunami. I uncrossed my arms and let my hands sit on my lap, studying the way they shook slightly. Rowan was a lot of things, but a liar wasn't one of them. Then again, I'd never known my parents to be liars. My siblings. My grandmother. How many people were in on this? How many of them looked at me and saw the reason our family was split apart? I swallowed past the lump in my throat and then swallowed again when it tried to come back up.

"Does Sam know?"

His jaw clenched. It took me a second to remember that I'd made him think I was dating his brother. If he were truly my boyfriend, I probably would have already known that answer. Nevertheless, it all seemed too small and insignificant—the fake relationship, the running away from him all this time, the anger. And yet, it was what I'd settled on, and once I did something, I didn't undo it. I didn't know how.

"I don't know if Sam knows."

"Thanks for telling me. I have to go." I slid out of the booth and gathered my things. He waved the ripped-out page.

"Sure you don't want to keep this one?"

"Positive."

Once I ripped something out, I never took it back. But I hadn't ripped him out of my life, had I?

CHAPTER NINE

TESSA

Past

I WATCHED Camryn saunter around the Hawthorne's expansive lawn like a lioness on the hunt. From the way she looked at Rowan, it was clear who the target was. She walked over to where he was entertaining his crew friends, squeezed in right beside him, and said something that made his friends laugh. My eyes were still on Rowan. It had only been a couple of hours since those lips, which were spread into a full-fledged grin, and been on mine—and a whole month since the first kiss at my grandma's party. The group laughed at something again, and Rowan looked down at Camryn. He flashed her that wide and welcoming smile that had jealously bleeding through me.

I pushed off the spot I'd been standing in most of the night and walked in the opposite direction, stopping when I found Celia and Freddie talking to Sam.

"Where have you been?" Celia asked, looking up. "With Ro?"

"No. Just . . . around. What are you guys doing?"

"Wishing we were elsewhere." Her comment had both Freddie and Sam chuckling.

"We were talking about taking the boats out tomorrow afternoon," Sam said.

"Hm." I glanced away, my eyes finding Rowan again. Camryn had her arms around his left arm, clinging on to him like a goddamn koala. My patience ticked. Couldn't she just keep her hands to herself?

"Tessa."

I blinked up at my sister. "What?"

"Why are you so distracted? Don't tell me you like one of the guys in Rowan's crew-crew." Celia smiled wide.

I rolled my eyes. I hadn't mentioned the kiss we'd shared. I almost had on two separate occasions, but held back. For some reason, it felt like something I wanted to protect and keep to myself. I also hadn't told her about all of those times I'd snuck out of my house to meet with him, or how many other kisses we'd shared, or the way we passed notes back and forth during AP Lit.

"I've been in a car with all of them at four in the morning, and trust me, they're disgusting," I answered, not thinking about how those four in the morning voyages had gone from a truck full of friends to just me and Rowan and then Rowan and me stopping on the side of the road to have a make out session. I barely recognized this boy-crazy version of myself, though, in my defense, I wasn't boy-crazy. I was Rowan-crazy.

"So why do you keep looking over there like you're interested?" Freddie stood straighter, puffing out his chest.

"Why do you assume I'm looking at them?" They all just stared, waiting. "Fine. I was trying to figure out Camryn's game."

Sam scoffed. "Her game is 'marry a Hawthorne,' it doesn't matter which one."

Celia frowned. I felt my own face contort. "Why?" we both asked.

"Because it's what her parents have drilled into that pretty little head of hers."

"Yeah, but why?" Celia asked. "She has her own money."

"And her parents only trust a few men to keep it that way."

"Why is she not hitting on you?" Celia asked. "You're the cuter one."

Sam chuckled. "I'm not the outgoing one. Besides, she knows Ro is the numbers guy."

"You can be a numbers guy," Freddie said. "You're smarter than he is."

I watched the way Sam laughed off my sister's words and frowned at my brother's, as if he'd never in a million years thought of himself as smarter or cuter than his brother. I shook my head and wondered when they'd learn to see themselves clearly. My eyes landed on Rowan's group of friends, but I found that he was no longer standing there. Neither was Camryn. Uneasiness prickled through me.

"I think I'm ready to go," I said.

"I'll come with," Celia said, standing and following behind me. She linked her arm around mine. "You okay? You look weird."

"I feel weird," I admitted. "I think I'm getting sick."

As we walked, I scanned the yard for Rowan and came up

short. Maybe he went back inside. Maybe he went upstairs. As my sister and I rounded the corner of the house, we heard a giggle and then another and then a moan. We both stopped walking and met each other's wide-eyed gazes.

"Should we go back?" she whispered.

"I don't know."

A part of me wanted to run, terrified to continue down the path we were on. Scared of what we'd find on the other side of it. I looked over my shoulder again. I could go back to the party, but for what? I wasn't enjoying myself at all and now that Rowan was missing in action I really didn't want to stick around. I swallowed down my trepidation and pushed on. Celia followed my lead, toward our ATVs, which were parked on the side. We always parked them there because it was the closest to our house. We'd been doing it so long, that it was a known thing by now. Whoever was hiding out here either wasn't a frequent visitor or didn't care about the fact that at one point Celia, me, or Freddie would be forced to walk by them. We held our arms a little tighter, our steps light on the grass when we really should have been stomping so the people ahead had some warning.

I heard another sound and decided to push on. If Rowan was fooling around with another girl . . . oh my god, I wasn't sure my heart could handle that. We hadn't spoken about being exclusive. Actually, we hadn't spoken much at all. We'd just kissed and kissed and kissed. He hadn't even tried to go to second base with me. Still. If I rounded the corner and discovered his mouth on Camryn's I thought I would die. I pushed on nonetheless, my heart hammering with each step I took, preparing for the worst. I tried closing my eyes to make out the sound better, but I couldn't. It sounded like someone was whining. It was definitely a whine, and it definitely came from Camryn. Finally, we reached the corner of the house. I was breathing heavier then, almost out of control. I looked at my sister, raised my chin as if to say *please look for me.* She frowned, confused, but I saw the clarity in her eyes. She understood what I wasn't saying. She was my sister, after all.

She looked, stood there stunned for a moment, and then turned back to me. I couldn't take it anymore. I took a step forward and looked for myself. My jaw dropped. Rowan was leaning against the wall, hands in his pockets. Camryn was standing in front of him between his legs. She wasn't flush against him, but she might as well have been. She was standing way too close for my comfort. It took my brain a moment to compute what the rest of my senses were already feeling. A sense of disgust curled through me at the sight of them.

My sister held my arm and tugged me in the direction of the door. We made noise, our feet speeding up a touch as Celia practically dragged me in the direction of our ATVs. Rowan looked up, instantly dropping his foot from the wall and standing straight at the sight of me. I looked from him to Camryn, who smiled.

"Bye, Tessa. It was good seeing you again," she said. Something in her eyes was telling, almost triumphant. It was as if she was winning some kind of game I wasn't sure I'd ever wanted to play in the first place.

With one last tug from Celia, I tore my eyes from them and moved, leaving them behind. My sister straddled the ATV, and I slid on behind her, hugging her middle and pressing the side of my face to her back.

"I didn't know you liked him like that," she said.

I pressed my face tighter against her back and reminded myself that I didn't like him like that. I couldn't. The silent ride gave me a moment to try to sort out my feelings. Rowan was a friend. Sure, we'd hooked up, but it hadn't meant anything. I repeated the words to myself, hoping they'd keep my heart from ripping apart.

We were halfway to our front door when we heard the familiar zoom of a dirt bike. We turned around at the same time and spotted Rowan expertly getting down, kicking the stand in place and taking off his helmet at the same time. He threaded his fingers into his hair in effort to fix it, but all it did was add to his disheveled sex appeal.

"We need to talk," he said as he stomped forward. I looked over my shoulder at Celia, whose eyes were wide as she turned around and unlocked the door.

"Fill me in later," she said quietly as she stepped inside.

I felt myself panicking, my heart throbbing a bit faster, my brain mushing over small details, like the fact that I'd just seen him standing way too close to Camryn and here he was not even two minutes later asking to speak to me. I wanted to shout it to the world. Instead, I crossed my arms as I stood on my porch, my heart thrashing with each step he took toward me.

"What are you doing here?"

"What you saw . . . what—" He exhaled when he reached me. I blinked up to his face. What I saw . . . him kissing Camryn. I swallowed my pride and hoped I would be able to summon a few words.

"We were never serious. We were never . . . anything. It's fine." I kept my voice as neutral as I could over the whooshing of blood in my ears.

"No." He stepped forward, looming over me, his chest almost crashing against mine. I arched my neck to meet his gaze as he cupped the side of my face. "It isn't fine. I don't want you to think that after we . . ." He shook his head, looked up at the sky as if searching for answers.

"I've seen you with plenty of girls. You've never apologized before."

"We hadn't spent nearly every waking moment together before." He shot me a look. "Don't pretend that meant nothing."

"I'm not pretending anything. I wasn't the one doing whatever it was you were doing with Camryn. Besides, we're just friends, aren't we? I wasn't expecting anything between us to change."

"What if I want change?"

"With me or with Camryn?"

"I didn't do anything with her," he said. "I swear. I didn't. Nothing happened. She was talking to me about something private, pulled me aside. We kept talking. I told her I was with someone and wasn't interested."

I searched his eyes, hoping for truth. I'd never known him to be a liar or a cheater, for that matter, but my heart was still unsettled, ricocheting all over the place.

"I want to believe you."

"I would never lie to you."

"I know how you are with Camryn, and I'm going to play second string to her."

"You would never be second to anyone, Tess."

"She was standing really close to you." I swallowed, trying to keep myself together, but I felt the tears clogging my throat. I'd never felt so vulnerable because of a guy.

"She's just . . . pushy and I'm an idiot. I should never have let her lead me away from the party."

"You don't even know how to have a relationship," I whispered. "You get a new girlfriend every day."

"I know, and I understand why you'd be hesitant, but I've never felt this connection with anyone." He closed his eyes briefly and shook his head. When he opened them again, he seemed to have made up his mind about something. "I want to change for you. Only for you. And I know it's only a matter of time before I leave for college, but you're going to graduate early. Maybe you can come to Columbia. Maybe we can take this change with us?"

"Yale," I said. "I've always wanted to go to Yale."

"Maybe Yale, maybe Columbia." His lips tugged. "Does that mean you want to try?"

I didn't know the answer to that. What would change bring? I didn't want to be the girl who followed her sort-of boyfriend to college or the girl who gave up her own dreams to follow a guy's. I didn't want to be the girl who fell for Rowan, and God knew he was easy to fall for with his warm blue eyes, killer body, and untamed hair.

For me, it was everything underneath that he would make me fall for, and I'd fall hard. His charm and his wit and the way his mouth moved into a secretive smile when he had a comeback he didn't think you'd handle well would grab ahold of me and never let go. He didn't allow me to respond. He took whatever expression was on my face as permission to bring his lips to mine. I saw my future flash before me in anticipation of his lips—the white picket fence and the kids, the dogs and the holidays around the tree. I'd never considered marriage, let alone children. The thought rocked me to my core, threatened to freak me out, but then his fingers thrust into my hair, and his tongue invaded my mouth in a sensual sweep that made my knees buckle.

I fell into the kiss, grabbing on to the front of his jacket and tugging him fully against me. This was what people spent their lives searching for. This scary, upside down feeling that made them feel as if they were on the brink, between their first and last breath. I'd always held on to the notion that I'd rather be alone than sparkless, but since I'd tasted the sparks, I had been afraid they'd be strong enough to make me implode.

CHAPTER TEN

TESSA

Present

"DID you know Dad sold the company in order to put me through school?" I asked Grandma Joan as soon as I walked through her door.

"Oh, dear." She glanced at me over her reading glasses. "Who told you?"

"Doesn't matter. Why didn't you?" I took a seat across from

her, watching as she poured tea into the second cup and slid it over to me.

"Because you would have dropped out."

"I would've found another way to pay for school. I could've transferred. It isn't like I needed to graduate from that specific school."

"You dreamed of going there your entire life."

"Because we had money and I thought it was possible, not because . . ." I shook my head and stopped talking as tears swam in my eyes. I blinked in an effort to hold them back, but then Grandma Joan slid her hand over mine, and it was no use. "I feel responsible."

"You aren't."

"I'm the reason Mom and Dad became so unhappy they decided they couldn't live together," I said. "You have to see that. The reason Mom filed for divorce and is dating a man young enough to be my brother. The reason one of the most hardworking, respectable families there was is suddenly no more."

"This was exactly why we didn't tell you. It's exactly why you need to take that opportunity in Paris."

"I never said I wasn't going to take Paris," I said with a little too much defiance in my voice. I swallowed and toned it down a bit. "I'm sorry. I'm just . . . I feel lied to."

"You were lied to for a good reason."

"Does Celia know?" I closed my eyes. God. If my siblings knew I would really feel like an asshole. I understood on some level that it wasn't my call, but it made me feel responsible. Our parents couldn't handle the debt or the sale of the company and it broke them. Our entire family split apart because of this. Because of me and my stupid little girl dream to go to Yale when, really, I could have gotten my degree anywhere. I got degrees in fashion design and marketing, neither of which was going to change the world, but they did change my life and not for the better thus far. I said this aloud. Grandma Joan tisked.

"You're not looking at the bigger picture," she said. "None of this is your fault. Did debt put a strain in your parents' marriage?" She shrugged. "Probably. That doesn't mean it's the reason the marriage fell apart."

It was true. A part of me knew and believed it. The other part, the childish one that wanted to hold on to the idea that her parents would be married until one of them died, wanted to continue to argue.

"How long is the apprenticeship in New York versus Paris?" she asked, veering off the subject.

"They're both one year."

"Both paid."

I nodded. Took a sip of coffee. "Both paid."

"I saw Rowan the other day."

I blinked at the sudden change of subject. "Yeah, he's been around."

"Have you seen him?"

"A few times."

"And? Any sparks?"

I smiled and glanced away, but didn't answer.

"Mm-hmm."

"He thinks I'm dating Sam," I blurted out.

"You little devil." Her face was priceless before she started to laugh but then sobered. "What ever happened to that blonde girl you didn't get along with? Camryn."

"Who knows." It was a lie. I lurked on Camryn's Insta here and there. You know what they say about enemies and all that jazz. "She travels a lot."

"Hm. I never liked that girl."

"She has that effect on people."

"What does that boy see in her?" Grandma Joan shook her

head in distaste. I'd cried to her once when Rowan was already away in college because I'd heard Camryn had finally made her move and made it count. I wasn't sure if the rumors were one hundred percent true, but it didn't matter. The fact that they were swirling was enough to hurt. "He's the whole package. She's . . ."

"Hot, blonde, smart, and slutty." I shrugged. She was. Nothing wrong with any of those qualities.

Sooner or later, she'd settle down, and she'd been wanting to do it with Rowan for so long I was sure it would happen. He and I had a fling. A short, temporary fling. That was all. I needed to keep categorizing it as such to keep my head right. We'd never work. Besides, he'd have a new love in his life soon: Hawthorne Industries. Making money was his first love. Any woman he settled down with would always be his mistress. Women like Camryn were okay with that because it was what they saw growing up. She'd doll up and accompany him to galas and be perfectly content spending her day at the spa and the mall on his dime. Nothing wrong with that either. I said this to Grandma Joan and shot her a look, daring her to trash talk. She'd been Camryn in her day. She knew better than to say anything distasteful, but in true Joan form, she spoke up anyway.

"That life gets old quickly. Soon she'll be luring the help or his colleagues to bed while he spends his nights at the office." She shot me a look of her own. "Trust me, I know."

What a life she'd lived, my grandma. She'd been every woman's nightmare back in her day and offered no apologies for it. Grandma had inherited a nice chunk of money from her first husband and a winery from my grandpa. I wasn't sure how one got tired of inheriting successful companies, but I wasn't about to find out. I was content living the lavish life vicariously through Celia. My phone vibrated, and to my surprise, I realized someone was actually calling me. I glanced at the screen and saw a picture of Rowan that I'd taken six years ago. He looked so . . . different. I hesitated, my hand on the phone.

"Answer his call, dear. Men like that don't wait."

I hit the red button and sent the call to voice mail. I knew my worth. It wasn't my fault that he hadn't seen it.

CHAPTER ELEVEN

I'D ALWAYS HEARD that your formative years are everything before the age of eight. I was sure that held at least some truth, but I was twenty-one when my parents suddenly split up, and it rocked all of us to the core. Maybe they weren't lovey dovey all the time, but they never seemed unhappy and divorce was supposed to be for unhappy couples that reached the end of the road and didn't see a reason to turn around together. Celia, Freddie, and I had sat side by side as they broke the news, Dad's breath full of liquor as his feelings poured out of him. He loved us more than anything but was no longer in love with Mom. Mom cried, dabbed her eyes with one of Dad's old-fashioned handkerchiefs, and said the same.

"This has nothing to do with the company," Mom added.

We all had known it was bullshit. Bull-fucking-shit.

In the years following their split, I had buried myself in schoolwork and graduated at the top of my class. It had been my way of not dealing. Not that it had helped, because here I was again, feeling lost and afraid in a way I hadn't felt often in my life. I'd had everything mapped out for me since I was a girl. We all had. And then *boom*, it all shattered, just like that. I looked around my room and sighed. There was no noise outside, no loud arguments or doors slamming, no laughter or music. It was just me in this big-ass house. As a teenager, I would have reveled in that.

I buried my face in my pillow and tried not to think about it. When I was sure I wasn't going to cry, I pushed myself up, grabbed my phone, and headed downstairs. I called my sister in London and fell into a fit of tears the moment she answered. I poured it all out there and apologized.

"What are you apologizing for?"

"Have you not been paying attention?" I snapped. "The reason mom and dad split up was because they couldn't handle paying for Yale and everything else."

Celia was quiet for a beat before she laughed. "I hope you're joking."

"I'm not. Grandma said it too. Well, sort of said it. It doesn't matter. I feel responsible."

"Well, don't. The moment you left for college mom and dad were at each other's throats. Trust me. I know. Why do you think I moved into that shithole apartment in the Bronx? They were miserable and it had nothing to do with you, so wipe your tears and move on. It isn't your fault, and Freddie and I don't blame you for it, either, so don't go thinking that."

I let that sink in and took a deep breath. "Okay. Thank you."

"Is that what you were calling me for?"

"Well, that and I'm pretty sure the house is ready to list. I know we all talked about it briefly, but I think it's time. I'm leaving soon so unless Dad comes back again or Mom comes in or one of you—"

"Hell no," she interrupted. "Let's conference call and get this over with."

She added Freddie, who was in Boston, and he called Mom, who was in France. Last, we added Dad, who was in Port Townsend.

"What time is it?" Dad grumbled. "Did anyone die?"

"No, but you will if you don't listen to what they have to say," Mom snapped.

"Who's going to kill me? Your pre-school-aged boyfriend?"

I cringed at my father's words. Freddie and Celia exploded with laughter.

"You guys might as well still be married," Freddie said, his deep voice taking over the call.

"I'm calling because I'm done with my portion of the house stuff. Everything except my room furniture and the barstools in the kitchen are in storage," I said. "So, should I call the realtor tomorrow?"

Everyone stayed quiet for a beat.

"You shouldn't do this on your own," Mom said, but her voice was soft, wary.

"Are you going to come home and help?"

"Not right now," she said.

"I say go for it," Dad said. "We can use the money and start something with it."

"You're always thinking about money," Mom pointed out.

"He has a point, Mom. You're comfortable because Grandma Joan saved the day, but Dad sold everything and used the money for necessities," Celia said. I wondered if she'd still sound so supportive if she knew where a chunk of the money had actually gone. Guilt nestled into my chest, splayed out there and chilled.

"Fine, call a realtor," Mom agreed. "Give him my information for any paperwork I'll have to sign. Make sure they have your Grandma's information as well, just in case you leave before anything happens."

"Of course, she'll leave before anything happens. Houses don't sell in a week," Dad said.

"You'd be surprised," Mom argued.

"Okay. Good talk," Freddie said. "I need to get back to work."

"Where are you right now anyway?" I asked. I'd called him a few times, and he always dodged the question, but if any of the people on the line knew where he was, they'd spill the beans for sure. I waited and pressed the phone closer to my ear. No one said anything. It was as if we were all waiting for the same thing.

"Working," he said simply. "Love you all. See you in Thanksgiving."

"At," I said.

"Whatever. At. It doesn't matter. Too many Native Americans died for us to just sit around the table, ignoring that fact while we dig into dry-ass turkey. I hate that holiday."

"Me, too," I agreed.

"Me, three," Celia said.

"Me, four," Dad added.

"So why do we even celebrate it?" Mom sounded as if she was about to cry. "Is this your way of telling me I won't be seeing any of my children this year?"

I exhaled. "I'll be there. Not sure where there is, but wherever you guys decide to meet, I'll go."

"Same."

"Same."

"Same."

I smiled. "I'll give you details on what the realtor says." I'd call my mom privately and ask her if she still wanted a small cottage near Grandma Joan's. She'd mentioned it in passing, but I wasn't sure if it was one of those things she just said or if she meant it.

"Thanks, baby," Dad said.

"Thanks, Sissy," Celia added.

"Gotta go," Freddie said and disconnected.

I hung up the phone and readied quickly, dressing as if I was going to a business meeting, even though I had no set destination just yet. Surely there must be at least a dozen realtors nearby. I always saw the open house signs scattered around. My heels clicked on the marble floor as I headed downstairs and into the kitchen. I started a pot of coffee, set a pan with some oil on the stove to fry some eggs, and had just popped two slices of bread into the toaster when the doorbell rang. I nearly dropped my jam.

I looked around the kitchen and put a timer on just in case. The last thing I wanted was for the oil to get too hot and for the entire house to smell like smoke. As I walked to the door, I tried to figure out if the insurance coverage was worth the potential jail time. I opened the door, my mind still on jail and whether or not the food was as bad as they said it was when my breath caught at the sight of Rowan on the other side. His hands were tucked into the black slacks he was wearing, his eyes as piercing as the blue tie around his neck. Why did he have to be so handsome with his perfectly brushed back hair and perfect body? And why the hell was he at my house? I gripped the door.

"What are you doing here?"

His head tilted. "You aren't going to invite me in?"

"No," I said. "How'd you know I was here?"

"This is your house, isn't it?"

I searched his face for a beat and realized he really had no clue what was going on in this house.

"Still. What do you—" The *beep, beep, beep* of the timer filtered through the house.

"Shit." I let go of the door and strode back to the kitchen, putting the toast on a plate and setting the bubbling oil aside for a moment. It had gone from not hot at all to too hot too quickly.

"You move impressively fast in those heels," Rowan said behind me.

"You want eggs?" I asked out of courtesy. He stayed quiet for a moment too long, so I turned and found him leaning against the threshold, his arms crossed, and a strange look on his face. "Is that a yes or no? Did you eat?"

"I . . . eggs would be great." He pushed off the jam and joined me, walking to the coffee machine and pouring two mugs. "You still take it black?"

"Like my soul."

He set the black one aside and poured a shit-ton of sugar and cream into the other. He glanced up at me, grinning. "One of us has to have one."

"Do you want your eggs scrambled?"

"Please."

"Ham? Cheese? Hot sauce?"

"My mouth is watering. I'll eat whatever you give me."

I smiled and got to work. Rowan watched me from the barstool and sipped his coffee. I kept my back toward him as I prepared his food in silence because the air was already charged with enough strange energy. Once I was finished, I set our plates down, leaving a chair between us. His arms were too long and sitting beside him when he was eating had always annoyed me.

"This is great," he said, stuffing more eggs into his mouth. "I could get used to this."

"You shouldn't, but I'm glad you like it."

He smiled, wiping his mouth on his napkin. "Where did the maid go?"

"We don't have one."

"Where's your sister? Freddie? Your dad?" He frowned, looking around. "I know your mom's in France."

"Everyone's gone."

"Who are you staying here with? Joan?"

"No. Joan has her own place, she'd never leave that hill."

Rowan stared, chewing slowly. "Why are you all dressed up?"

"I always dress like this. Not that you would know."

His lips twitched. "I'm used to seeing you in converse and ripped-up jeans."

"I'm used to seeing you in spandex." My face flamed as I thought about him in his rowing outfit . . . and halfway out of it. I'd seen pictures of a well-celebrated calendar that he and his rowing crew had been a part of. It was . . . impressive to say the least.

He chuckled softly. "You saw the calendar."

"Who *didn't* see the calendar? It was all anyone talked about."

"Does my brother know that you've been keeping tabs on me?"

"I haven't, and it doesn't matter."

"Of course it matters."

"Why's that?" I asked despite myself.

"Because it means you're still interested in me."

"Don't flatter yourself."

"I don't need to."

I rolled my eyes and took a bite of my toast, swallowing my snappy comeback. I didn't have time for this game today.

"Why isn't Sam staying with you?"

"Why would he be?"

"You have a huge empty house all to yourself, you're together now, why wouldn't he?" He raised an eyebrow. I realized two things: Sam hadn't told him the truth and Rowan was trying to call my bluff. Tough luck. I wouldn't budge on this.

"You're right. I'll invite him over tonight, tell him to pack a bag."

His jaw clenched. "Why him?"

"Why not?"

"Why him?" he asked again.

"Why her?" I fired back.

"Why do you keep bringing her up? Because of the rumors back in college?" He dropped his fork and ran both hands through his hair in an exhale. "It was never serious between us."

"It never is with you."

He stared at me a moment longer. Seconds ticked by. Minutes. My heart felt as if it were on a frantic free fall from the highest rollercoaster imaginable. I hated that I felt this pull between the two of us, hated that it had to be him to make me feel this way every time. I broke the staring contest first, and he stood and gathered our plates before taking them to the sink and washing them while I sipped my coffee. The entire exchange may have been the most domestic thing to ever occur in this kitchen, argument and all. The thought made my heart heavy.

"So, where to?" he asked as he dried his hands and faced me.

"I need a realtor."

"I thought you wanted to get out and never come back."

"We're selling the house."

He blinked. "This house?"

"We don't have another one that I'm aware of. Unless you want to drop some more knowledge on me while I'm in town."

"You love this house."

I shrugged. "What is love anyway?"

He looked as if he wanted to say something but just shook his head. I hated when he left my curiosity scrapping for more, but I wouldn't give in to it this time. I'd purged and wasn't allowing myself any luxuries.

"Do you know any realtors?" he asked.

"No. Do you?"

"A few. Want me to make some calls?"

"No, thank you. I'm sure you're busy. You're all dressed for work and stuff," I said and then frowned. "You never told me why you came by."

"You didn't answer my call yesterday."

"You called *once*."

"And you didn't answer."

I laughed. "You call someone one time and then show up at their place if they don't answer? This is something that women are actually okay with?"

"I wouldn't know. I don't call people unless I'm interested in doing business with them or fucking them."

My heart launched hard against my chest. "Oh. Are you trying to hire me?"

"Not exactly." His smile was sinful. "Although, I do have a job if you want one."

"Want and need are two entirely different concepts," I said. "I know they're entirely foreign to you, but you should become familiar with them just in case."

"I'll be sure to do that," he said. "Do you need one?"

I hesitated. "I'm only here for two weeks."

"You'll probably be more efficient than half the people there in those two weeks."

I pulled my bottom lip between my teeth and peered up at him. I had a little money socked away, but I could definitely use the extra cash just in case. "What positions are available?"

"I need an assistant."

"An assistant?" My eyes widened. Work in close quarters with him? "Absolutely not."

"Why not? It's only temporary. The assistant I hired bailed on me yesterday, and I need to start going into the office to sort shit out, but I can't do that and book appointments. I could use someone I trust." He paused, watching my reaction.

Having Hawthorne on my resume would look pretty good, even if it were only a two-week assistant job.

Don't do it. He kissed you the other day and awakened things you hadn't thought about in years. He's here because he clearly wants to fuck you, and that will never end well. Don't do it.

"So, I'd be doing you a favor." I heard myself speak, but I hadn't meant to. It was as if my brain and my heart were having an invisible tug-of-war and my heart was winning by a mile.

"Huge favor." His eyes glittered in a way that made me shift from one foot to the other.

"What's your position?"

"Officially? CFO."

"Well, la-di-dah." My brows rose. "Must be nice."

His expression soured. Rowan hated talking about things like that. "Do you want the assistant position or not?"

"When would I start?"

He eyed me up and down. I tried not to let that sweep affect me. "You can start right now."

"I need to find a realtor."

"You can make some calls from the office."

My heart pounded. "Okay."

CHAPTER TWELVE

ROWAN

I HIRED her before thinking it through. I seemed to do that a lot where she was concerned. Still. I could use the help. I hadn't lied about that.

"How much are you paying me for this?" she asked from the passenger seat.

"Well, I'm doubling as your taxi driver right now, so that should shave off a few bucks."

She sputtered out a laugh. "Nice try, hot shot."

My heart did a little dip. I glanced over at her and couldn't help but smile. I knew I needed to take things slowly with her. If I didn't, she'd chop my head off and run away. At the first sign of discomfort, she would run. At least she used to. I reminded myself that I didn't know this Tessa well enough yet.

When I reached the stoplight, I studied her profile. She was so goddamn beautiful and she didn't even know it.

"Did you sketch any more dresses yesterday?"

"Just the one."

"Are you still sketching furniture?"

Her smile was slow and wide. "Here and there."

Here and there. That meant she had a drawer full of sketches no one but her had ever seen. I'd kill to see the room, the drawer, and have her show me the sketches. That ship sailed long ago, though.

Camryn, I reminded myself. Fucking Camryn and the stupid rumors she'd spread. Not that they'd all been completely false. Unfortunately.

"I'd love to see them."

"Maybe." She looked over at me as I pulled into the parking lot. "So, you'll tell me what I need to do, right?"

"Yes, and I'll walk you to HR so that they can discuss payment with you."

She shrugged. "I mean, I'm only here for two weeks. Is it worth me filling out all the paperwork?"

I parked and turned toward her. "What happens in two weeks?"

"I check out both locations and pick what apprenticeship I'm taking."

"Hm. New York or Paris. What companies are offering the apprenticeships?"

A small smile splayed on her lips. "Wouldn't you like to know?"

She got out of the car and sauntered toward the front of the building. I gave myself two, three seconds to look at her ass before I got out of the car and jogged over to her.

"I would like to know." In truth, I was dying to know, but I wasn't sure why. I chalked it up to curiosity.

We walked toward the building. It wasn't a big high-rise by any means. It was only four stories, but every floor was filled to the max. After buying Monte from Tessa's family, we were able to secure their office building and their factory. It was important to her father that the employees kept their jobs, and my dad agreed with that, but that meant we had to house more employees than we had room for. We walked to HR, where I quickly explained Tessa's position and salary, and then told them to prepare the papers.

When we walked by the marketing area, Samson's head snapped up from his computer. He frowned at the sight of Tessa beside me. I watched him closely, noting the way his eyes said something to her and hers said something back to him.

They had a wordless, two-second conversation, and even though I only caught one end of it, I decided they were both full of shit. Maybe I didn't know my brother the way I once did. Maybe we weren't on the best terms anymore, but I knew when a man was in love with a woman, and this wasn't it. Annoyance ripped through me. Why would they lie to me about something so stupid? It made no sense. Still. It didn't change the fact that if they were lying, my brother was an asshole. If they weren't lying, he was a bigger asshole because he was trying to get under my skin. I placed my hand on her elbow to guide her in the direction of my office, made the introduction between her and the people who worked in that area, and then lead her into my office, shutting the door behind us.

"Why did you lie to me about Sam?"

Her eyes widened slightly as she took a step back. "What?"

I didn't repeat myself. She knew I wouldn't. I kept my hands balled at my sides in an effort to keep from reaching out to her. What I wanted to do was grab her arms, push her back against my door, and kiss that surprised look right off her face. The way she molded against me during our kiss the other day hit me in a flash, and I felt myself harden in my slacks. I wondered if she knew how she affected me. Probably not.

"Lie to you about what exactly?" she asked. "Being with him?"

"Yes."

She shook her head, smiling. "What do you want us to do? Jump each other every chance we get? He respects my space, and I respect his. He is at work, you know?"

I watched her for a moment and decided that I didn't believe her. Maybe I just didn't want to. Something was going on there. Maybe they were just hooking up; I wanted to punch the thought away. The door opened behind her before I could question her further, and my father peeked his head in, his lips pulling into a welcoming smile when he saw Tessa.

"My girl, it's been so long."

"Al. Always a pleasure."

He stepped in and gave her a warm, albeit quick hug. Dad wasn't a touchy-feely kind of guy, but he'd always loved Tessa. "What brings you by?"

"I need a new assistant."

Dad glanced up. "Again? This is what, assistant number three in one summer? What the hell are you doing, Rowan?"

"I don't know."

"Well, fix it," Dad said sternly. His features softened when he turned to Tessa. "Don't let him scare you away, and if he tries, you come talk to me."

"I will." She smiled. It was a smile she hadn't directed at me in four and a half years. The realization shook me.

"I spoke to your father the other day. He keeps inviting me up to go fishing. Have you been?"

"I visited last summer. It's truly beautiful out there. So peaceful."

"A lot of wineries, too, I heard."

She nodded. "We visited one. It was breathtaking."

"I'd love to hear about it. Maybe I can plan my visit around fishing and wine."

"Hey, you don't need much more than that," Tessa said, smiling. Dad chuckled. I stared dumbfounded. In five minutes, she managed to turn him into a nineties-sitcom father. He was a no-good father, no-good person I reminded myself. He was a cheater, a liar, a user. He was a fake. Even Tessa had to see through his act.

I was still stuck firmly in disbelief when he turned to me, saying, "Rowan, I'll be expecting you in my office in five minutes." Then he turned and left, shutting the door behind him.

Tessa turned to face me. "So, do I get a desk?"

"It's right behind you."

She pivoted slightly, looked, and then turned back to me wide-eyed. "We're sharing an office?"

She looked so absolutely horrified that I stifled my urge to laugh.

"We are."

"Did the last three assistants have to share an office with you?"

No, but she didn't need to know that. "I already told you, we're running out of space."

She blinked, looking exasperated. "This is crazy."

"It's only two weeks."

"Right. You're right." She dropped her hand. "Two weeks."

"Look through the Rolodex on my desk. I should have some realtors in there."

"Oh my god, you have a Rolodex?" She brought her hand up to try to stifle her laugh, which didn't work. What escaped her lips was loud and full of mirth. The sound stirred something inside me, and I found myself laughing right along with her.

"It keeps things neat."

"Neat," she squeaked, laughing harder. "You can keep things neat on your smart phone or computer."

"A Rolodex is a perfectly fine tool. It's alphabetized and easy to use." I felt myself scowl. "Besides, I don't want my secretaries going through my smartphone or computer."

"Oh my god. You're such a dork." She was still laughing lightly as she said it. "Do your admirers know how big of a nerd you are under all those hot muscles?"

"I don't know. Are you one of my admirers?" I grinned as I watched the expression on her face morph from amusement to complete embarrassment. She looked away. When she looked at me again, she'd already schooled her expression into one that screamed haughty attitude.

"Isn't your dad waiting for you?"

Shit. He was. He hated waiting. I looked at her a second longer, wishing she'd drop pretenses and let me read an unfiltered expression. She wouldn't, and I knew it. I begrudgingly walked out of my office and headed toward my dad's. I took a breath when I reached it, knocked once, and pushed the door open. I sat across from him, crossing my ankle over my knee as I waited for him to finish his phone call.

"Tessa Monte, huh?" he said, raising an eyebrow as he ended the call.

"She's only here for two weeks and needed a job."

"And you, being the selfless man that you are, decided to give her one." He tilted his face, no sign of emotion in his eyes, and looked at me for a moment too long. I tried not to wither under his stare. My dad had a way of looking at you that made you think he was jumbling through your deepest, darkest secrets. Probably because he had so many of his own.

"Let's not talk about selfless," I responded, raising an eyebrow.

"I never claimed to be selfless."

"Neither did I."

He shut his mouth and stared at me for a moment, seemingly thinking about what his next words would be. I loved seeing my father tongue-tied. His extramarital affairs would forever give me the upper hand in arguments because he was the one with two families, not me. He was the one who had been hiding an illegitimate child with his longtime secretary, the one my mother had thrown a lavish baby shower for. The one we all went to visit at the hospital after her sob story of the man who impregnated her bouncing when he found out about it. Disgust settled into the pit of my stomach.

"I understand you're still upset—"

"I will always be upset. I'll never forgive you for what you did to Mom."

"One day you will," he said calmly. My eyes widened. Who was this man? Where was the man who stood up and lashed out when challenged?

"I won't."

"One day, you'll see that not everything in life is black and white."

"And that gray area extends to the vows you made?" I asked. "If it had been Mom cheating with some man, having his child, would you expect me to be okay with it?"

"Of course not."

"But it's okay because you're the man."

"No, son." He exhaled, closing his eyes. "It's never okay, but your mother and I have been over for ten years. We've been going through the motions, staying together for the sake of the company, for pretenses. Mari—"

"Don't say her name." My jaw clenched. I swallowed thickly. I hated Mariah. I'd put entirely too much time into helping that woman, only to find out it had all been a fucking lie. That was what happened when a parent was unfaithful the way my father had been. It wasn't only the wife who blamed herself, the children did too. What did we do to deserve this? Could we have been better and prevented it?

"When you get married—"

"I didn't come here for a lecture on marriage and love, and if I had, you'd be the last person I listened to," I spat.

He shook his head, the expression in his eyes hardening. "Well, then, I guess it's a good thing I'm not asking you to marry anyone for love."

"I don't believe in love or marriage," I said. "So, we're safe on both accounts."

"In that case, don't involve her more than she needs to be. Your mother always felt she was a bad choice for you, and now that we're in this situation, if you do what you're supposed to and marry someone who knows what's expected and will abide by the contract, you should leave that girl out of it. If that person is Camryn or someone like that, she will make her life a living hell, and Tessa has been through enough these last few years."

"And you would know," I said, though, my brain was still stuck on his words. My heart stirred uneasily. *"Your mother hates her for you."*

"I speak to both her parents regularly, so yes, I would know," he said. "Those people are hurting."

"And suddenly you're Pope fucking Francis."

He glared. "Don't use that kind of language if you're going to talk about the Pope."

"Oh, I'm sorry. I forgot that you've found your faith again." I put my hands up. "Please continue, I shouldn't be friends with Tessa, shouldn't give her a job, because you think what? I'm going to fuck her and hurt her, is that it?"

"I didn't say that."

"It's what you did with Mariah, isn't it? You gave her a job as your assistant, fucked her, and got her pregnant? Oh, but wait, I'm not married yet, so I don't need to sit through this bullshit."

"This is a useless conversation to have with an immature child," he muttered. "This is why I'd rather have your brother take over the company. At least he has his head on straight."

"You want him to take over the company so you can control him." I jolted out of my chair and gripped the edge of the desk. "You know as well as I do that he'd let this company drown, but be my guest, maybe you should call him in here to discuss your business instead of me."

"Maybe I already have," he said with a cool air that could freeze the poles.

I pushed off the desk and left his office, not caring that we hadn't actually discussed the day's agenda as I slammed the door behind me. As I walked back to my own office down the hall, I caught a few wary eyes on me and knew they had heard me yelling.

I didn't care.

CHAPTER THIRTEEN

TESSA

I WATCHED as Rowan stalked toward me with a look I knew well. He was pissed, his body language practically screaming for people not to talk to him, look at him, or think about him. I thanked the realtor and hung up the phone just as he walked through the door, then I swiveled my chair to face him as he rounded his desk and sank in his chair with a heavy sigh. I waited, studied the way his features went through the motions: pissed off, disbelief, pissed off again. Deciding to leave him alone to his sulking, I turned around, wishing I had access to the monologue bouncing around in his head. At the very least, it would be entertaining. Alistair Hawthorne had always been kind to my family and me, but he sucked at being a father, telling the guys they were unwanted and a mistake on more than one occasion. That their mother had tricked him into getting her pregnant – twice. It was ridiculous but I could see the light leave Sam's eyes whenever he spoke about it. He hadn't divulged much about his parents' divorce, but I was sure some of the cloud that passed over Rowan's face had something to do with that, though I couldn't imagine why. It's not like either one of them had ever seemed in love, or happy for that matter.

I clicked the mouse and powered up the sleeping computer once more, checking out the realtor's website. Why did realtors put their face on everything? I shook my head and clicked on his face. He looked like a supermodel, which could have been why he wanted to put his face on everything.

"What's so funny?"

I glanced over my shoulder to Rowan. "Nothing. Just looking at your friend Enrique's website. I think he has more pictures of himself than houses."

His lips twitched. "Did you speak to him?"

"Yep. We set up a meeting. Thank you," I said. I could tell he was still reeling from his conversation with his dad and wished I could say something to cheer him up, but I wasn't sure what.

"He's going to go check the house out?" he asked, a bitter tone in his voice again.

"Yep."

"At what time?"

"Five thirty."

He gave a nod and went back to his computer. The door opened, and Sam popped his head in.

"Hey."

"Hey." My smile widened at the sight of him.

"You got plans for lunch?"

"Not as of now."

"Meet me downstairs at twelve."

I gave him a thumbs-up and laughed at the moonwalk he did as he left. He was such a clown.

"Cute," Rowan said with a bite in his tone that made my attention whip toward him. He was leaning against his desk, legs casually crossed as he looked at me. I hadn't even heard him move.

"What is your problem?"

"Nothing. Just enjoying the show. You and my brother." He shook his head, full lips pursed as he pushed off the desk and walked over. My heart stalled, thinking he was coming over to me, but he just opened the file cabinet beside my desk. "So fucking cute."

"You should try to at least be cordial with him."

"Yeah, there's no chance of that happening now." He smiled like a shark, slow, powerful, and without humor. My heart thumped against my chest at everything he wasn't saying. He pulled out a file and shut the cabinet with a little rattle that made me jump.

"He's still your brother," I whispered.

"Yet, he knows no bounds." He pressed his palm onto my desk and leaned closer to me, crowding me in a way that made my pulse skitter with the awareness of him. "For the record, I hate the way he looks at you. I hate the way he talks to you and does a little show for you, and I hate how entertained you are by all of it."

"Rowan."

"I hate it," he breathed the words, his eyes dark and murky.

I realized then that I wasn't great at pretending at all. A part of me wanted to just flat-out tell him I'd lied. The other part of me screamed that it didn't matter. It was safer for him to think I was with someone else, anyway. I forced my eyes away from his, looked at the computer, and changed the subject.

"Is there anything you want me to help you with? What was the last secretary doing for you?"

He was quiet as he took his seat again. The slap of the file hitting his desk filled the air before he finally answered my question. "She alternated between Instagram and Facebook posts, but what she was supposed to be doing was confirming meetings for my upcoming trips."

"Do you have a list?"

"First drawer to your right. There are over five hundred companies on there, so I don't expect you to call every single one, but any meeting you can set up would help. Just make sure to coordinate the dates and locations accordingly."

My eyes widened as I scanned the first page, and when I looked back up, I knew my mouth was hanging open. "How many places are you planning to visit?"

"Well, I'll start in London and then head to Paris. I want to try to go to Africa and some places in South America as well, but those will be separate trips."

I felt my brows hike up. "Are you dedicating your entire year to this?"

"I guess so." He sighed, running a hand through his hair. The phone on his desk rang and interrupted our conversation, so I turned around and started going through the list and calling people while he worked. Between lunch with Sam and the work I had on my desk, the rest of the day flew by, and I thought maybe we could do this whole friendship slash work thing after all.

CHAPTER FOURTEEN

"THERE'S AN OFFICE PARTY THIS SATURDAY,"
Sam said.

We were lying in the lawn chairs by my pool. I was
tanning, he was reading. I wasn't sure what. Dennis Lehane's
latest if I had to guess. I shifted onto my stomach to tan
my back.

"And you're telling me this why?"

"Because you're part of the company right now and you
should come."

I scoffed. "I'm only there for two weeks. That hardly makes me part of the company."

Besides, I still wasn't over the idea that they were splitting it up or that Monte belonged to them. I wouldn't say this to Sam, though, because I loved him and didn't want to make him feel bad.

"Fine," he said. "I want you to go with me. Both of my parents will be there, and I have a feeling they'll take the opportunity to fill everyone in on what's happening."

"And you need me to hold your hand."

"It would be nice."

I frowned, turning onto my side and fixing my top so I didn't flash him. "You're serious."

"I am." He glanced over the book in his hands. "If you really don't want to go, it's okay. I just figured you were probably free anyway."

"Is it super fancy?"

"Not really. Cocktail attire. Little black dress and all that." He grinned. It was so similar to his brother's. A show-stopping grin, for sure, and Samson had a dimple to boot. I sat up.

"Fine. I'll go."

"You sound less than thrilled about this."

"Well, I don't want to go, but you already called me a loser for not having plans, and now I feel like I need to hold your hand."

He snorted out another laugh and went back to his book, but I wasn't done with the conversation yet.

"Why don't you already have a date to take?"

"I have the party, and the girl I'm kind of seeing isn't ready to meet my parents."

"Your mom's a vulture. I wouldn't introduce any girl to her."

He peeked over his paperback. "She got you that bad, huh?"

I shrugged, fell onto my back again, and threw an arm over my eyes.

"You know she has a twisted way of telling people she loves them, right?"

"If that was her way of telling me she loved me, I can't even imagine what hate must sound like spilling from her lips."

"Venomous."

"I bet she loves Camryn." I smirked and then looked over at him, eyes wide. "Will she be there?"

"I doubt it. I mean, she has no reason to go that I know of, but I don't talk to my brother, remember?"

"Why is that? You two used to be close." It was something that we rarely discussed and, before I'd started talking to Rowan again, I felt weird asking. I was always walking the fine line between wanting to know everything Ro was up to and not wanting to know anything at all.

"He thinks I'm in love with you and that I'm the reason you've been avoiding him for four years."

I let out a laugh and then sobered. "Wait, you're serious?"

"As a heart attack."

"Why would he . . ." I let my words hang. My heart pounded hard against my chest as Sam looked at me. Oh my god. Was he? I sat up quickly, gripping the edge of the chaise. "Are you?"

He closed his paperback with a *thump*. Didn't even bother marking the page. My heart plummeted. He couldn't be. We were friends. Such good friends. If he felt that way toward me, it would ruin everything. It already had between Ro and me. He grabbed the edge of the chaise he was sitting on and dragged it with him until our knees were touching.

"Sam," I whispered, emotion gripping my throat and squeezing. I shook my head to will the emotion away. He shrugged.

"Nope. Not in love with you."

I let out a laugh and slapped him. "You had me going."

"I mean, they say the way to know if you're in love with

someone is to kiss them," he said, his lips forming a slow smile. "We can give it a go."

"I prefer not to," I said, but his face was mere inches from mine when he moved forward. Finally, when he moved even closer, I held my breath, my fingers tightening on the edge of the chaise.

"Fuck it. I'm going for it," he whispered.

I could have stopped him, but I didn't, because how easy would it be to be in love with someone like Sam? Someone who would follow me around the world and take a job anywhere because he wasn't married to *this* company or *this* city. My heart pounded even harder. He leaned in, his lips brushing mine lightly before fully pressing them against mine. I felt nothing. Even as our tongues touched and danced, I felt nothing. We broke apart quickly and looked at each other.

His eyes searched mine for a beat. "You pulled away faster than people pull away in spin the bottle."

"I hate spin the bottle, and I didn't feel a need to continue to kiss you," I said, but my eyes were wide on his. "What does that mean?"

"Nothing." He shrugged. "It's like kissing a sister or something. No offense."

I exhaled heavily. "Oh, thank God."

The backdoor slammed, making us both making us jolt away from each other, and we turned to look at it. Rowan stood, arms crossed, beside a man I recognized as Enrique the realtor. I shot to standing and grabbed my maxi, pulling it over myself to cover up my bikini.

"That's the realtor."

"Yeah, Enrique," Sam said, nodding as he stood.

He grabbed his paperback and walked with me. With each step, I wondered how much of that they saw. Did Rowan see me kiss his brother? My stomach churned at the thought. A part of me wanted to be proud of it, but it just made me sick. My face was beet red by the time I stood close enough to make out both of their expressions. Enrique was smiling wide, hand out ready to greet me. Rowan's expression could freeze the ecosystem. I focused on Enrique, shaking his hand in introduction.

Sam spoke to him next, small talk I couldn't even pay attention to because I was so focused on my sandaled feet. I wouldn't dare look Rowan in the face. I felt his eyes on me, though, burning, questioning. Enrique and Rowan headed inside the house, and I nearly jumped when Sam grabbed my elbow.

"I'll see you later, gator," he said.

"Later, gator."

He walked away, saying his goodbyes to the guys as he went. When he got to the front door, he turned around and looked at me again. "Don't forget about Saturday."

"I won't."

I showed Enrique around, stood by while he took pictures, and spoke to him about the house. I fully intended to clear things up with Rowan. I wasn't sure whether or not he'd seen me with Sam outside, but if he had, I wanted him to know there was nothing going on there. Halfway through the tour, Rowan's phone rang, and with barely a goodbye, he was striding back through my front door. As I watched him leave, I vowed to tell him tomorrow at the office. Definitely tomorrow.

CHAPTER FIFTEEN

ROWAN HAD an early call with China, so Sam picked me up on his way to the office the following day. The truck was still being fixed, and I hadn't even thought about what I would do if I had to replace it. In truth, I didn't need it. If I took the apprenticeship in the city, I would use the subway. If I took it in Paris, I couldn't ship a car anyway, so I had no use for one over there. Sam said he would fix the truck and leave it at Grandma Joan's house as an option, which made sense since it had been my grandfather's truck first. When we got to the office, Rowan's car was already parked. My stomach dipped.

"Do you think he saw anything yesterday?" I asked.

"I think if he had seen anything, I would have a black eye right now."

I rolled my eyes. "Please."

"Don't get me wrong, I don't regret doing it, but I don't want to hurt him."

I agreed with that. We went inside and headed our separate ways. I took a moment outside of the closed office, debating between knocking and just walking in. I wasn't sure. I decided to knock. The door opened as if he'd been waiting for me. I opened my mouth to say just that when I saw Camryn standing there smiling. Her red lipstick was smeared. My stomach churned at the sight.

"Tessa, it's so nice to see you," she said, all cheerful. "I'm so glad you're helping Rowan these next couple of weeks. He's always so exhausted and—"

"Camryn," Rowan interrupted. "You can go now."

She shot him a glare. "Of course. I'll see you later." She smiled widely at me, and I watched as she sauntered away. Red was the only color my spotty vision would allow me to see as I shut the door behind her.

I didn't even look at Rowan as I sat and fired up my computer. My heart would shatter if I did. Seeing Camryn, her smeared lipstick, was enough to tell me that Rowan wasn't nearly as single as he claimed to be. It made me realize that things with him were a double-edged sword, regardless of when they began and ended or at which point in our lives we met up. As long as she was in the picture, there was no room for me. Before, I'd taken the couch and made room for myself. At this stage in my life, I didn't want the couch. I wanted the king-size bed. I wanted the assurances that it would be me, only me. And if I were being one hundred percent honest with myself, I didn't want that either. I was terrified to be on the bed. At least the couch gave me an easy exit.

I dove into the phone calls, placing them in rapid fire, *boom, boom, boom*, never once looking up to acknowledge him behind me. He didn't speak to me, either, and I was grateful that he was in one of his moods. The only time I saw him was when he left the office for his morning meeting, but I avoided looking at him when he came back. I even went as far as holding my breath when he walked by. I reminded myself that I had an apprenticeship I needed to choose and report to soon. That was what I needed to dedicate my life to. Not scary would-be feelings for a man who didn't have it in him to fully reciprocate them.

I WAS LOUNGING on my bed and made a pros and cons list for the New York company and Paris company. So far, New York was winning. Language and proximity to the majority of my family were the biggest factors. Celia was in London, but only temporarily, and Mom lived in France, but not close enough to Paris that I could stay with her. The thought of seeing her with a guy my age crossed my mind, and I shivered. My phone vibrated on my nightstand, making me sit up tall as I reached for it. I swiped the screen and read a text from Sam. Party canceled. Relief flooded through me.

Me: I don't want to say I'm relieved, but . . .

Sam: Thought you'd say that

Me: Srsly though, why cancel?

Sam: Something about letting employees know via email. They wanna meet with me and Ro instead.

Me: Prob should have done that to begin with.

When I didn't see any little dots that signaled him typing

back, I set my phone down and turned back to my list. The moment my pen hit the paper again, my phone started vibrating. I exhaled and lifted the phone to my ear, thinking it would be Sam again, except it was Freddie's voice I heard.

"Freddie?" My heart stopped. My brother never called me out of the blue.

"I need a favor."

"Oh." I paused, a sense of gratitude spread through me in knowing it was nothing serious but was immediately replaced with irritation. "You haven't even asked me how I'm doing. How are you? How's the job? How many men have you tortured today?"

"Two," he said without skipping a beat. I paused, gaping even though he couldn't see me.

"Seriously?"

I felt my eyes widen. My brother never, ever divulged information about his work with The Company. That's what he called his place of employment. I thought not re-enlisting in the military meant no more scary shit, but from what we'd heard about The Company, that didn't seem to be the case. They were constantly changing their identities in order to catch fugitives, that's what we'd gathered from the breadcrumbs Freddie fed us when we saw him.

"You asked."

"Jesus." I exhaled. "Were they bad people?"

"Aren't we all?" he said with a humorless chuckle. A chill ran down my spine.

"What's the favor?"

"Remember the little gallery on Main? I need you to go to an exhibition they're having. My paintings are featured, and I want you to tell me what prices are being offered."

"Isn't that gallery super exclusive?" I smiled. "That's a pretty big deal, Freddie."

"Yeah. I wanted to be there, but duty calls." The disappointment in his voice tugged at my heart.

"I'll be there and FaceTime you so you can experience it with me."

He chuckled. "They won't let you FaceTime in there. Just keep me posted."

Six hours later, I was walking into the gallery, making good on my promise.

CHAPTER SIXTEEN

ROWAN

SOMETIMES LIFE GIVES YOU LEMONS, but other times, it dumps buckets of shit over your head. It wasn't only my brother, me, and our parents in the meeting. My grandparents were sitting in as well. Ultimately, that was the kicker. At least we could argue with our parents. Sam and I wouldn't dare talk back to our grandparents, though. Hell, Dad didn't even have the guts to do that. Samson was staring at Grandpa Pete in complete and utter disbelief as he continued his rant about how irresponsible and unreliable our parents were.

"They had one job and that was to be the face of the

company. The face," Grandpa Pete said, raising his voice, "Not even the brains! And look where this got us. We've built a family company around two frauds."

"People get a divorce all the time, Pete," Mom said, her voice softer than I'd ever heard it.

"Divorce doesn't belong in Hawthorne Industries. Not if you're the face of the company."

"Dad—" My own Dad started. Grandpa shot him a look that made him hold his words, then looked over at me.

"You want this company? This is your shot at it. I already agreed to pay your parents a lump sum. If you want it, you need to find yourself a wife, someone you can boss around if need be. That's the clause in the contract," he said sternly. "I don't want to hear any hoopla about it. You either want this or you don't, which is it?"

"I want it." My voice was steady.

I'd practiced this scene over and over in my head growing up, the day they'd finally let me take the rein of the company. The day they'd finally let me lead. I hadn't planned on it being surrounding something like marriage, but if that's what it took I'd have to focus and convince myself to do it. I met my father's gaze. He didn't look happy. I wasn't sure if it was because he was being kicked out of the seat or because I would soon be filling it. He tilted his head as if to say, *what's the matter? Isn't this what you've been asking for? More responsibility, more independence, more of a say in the company. More, more, more.* My mother looked uncomfortable, as if finally realizing after all of these years just how much of a burden their expectations were to us.

"So, you're saying you'll give us the States, South America, and Europe accounts if we get married," Sam said, his voice hoarse.

"Only one of you has to marry," Dad clarified. "That's how it worked with me and Joe."

Grandpa scoffed. "The firstborn has to do it and you know it. Unless he's not up for the challenge."

"I never said I wasn't," I argued at the suspicious look Grandpa gave me. "It goes against everything I believe in, but I'm up for the challenge."

"Everything you believe in?" Grandpa let out a tense laugh. "It's marriage, not an abortion. You don't need a moral compass to do it."

"No, I suppose we don't need a moral compass at all," I said flippantly. Mom turned bright red. Dad's eyes narrowed.

"Marriage is a contract, just like any other," Dad responded.

"Stay out of this." My grandfather's words thundered in the silent room. "You've already shown you don't have a backbone."

I glanced at Samson. We had a wordless conversation that we hadn't had in years.

What the fuck is going on?

Our parents are insane.

What do we do?

Don't worry. I got this under control.

"Do you want the company or not?" Grandpa Pete pushed.

I held back a groan. "I just want to work."

"You were groomed for this," Dad reminded me, a hint of warning in his voice. My heart beat harder.

"I want it," I said finally.

I folded my napkin and put it on the table, leaning back. My grandmother, who hadn't gotten a word in before, finally spoke in that soft voice of hers, telling us how important this was to our company and our brand. Ultimately that was all we were to them – a brand. A place that hardworking families felt comfortable going to for fabrics and manufacturing. They wouldn't change their mind about that and if I wanted the company, which I did, I'd make a change in it down the line. I'd expand it, make money, and the moment I could, I'd buy it from them. In order to do that, I just had to do this one thing. One massive thing.

I'd never hated the fact that my grandparents started the company because ultimately without them there would be nothing. What bothered me was that they were the type of people who gave you things conditionally. Their love was conditional. Their support was conditional. Our roles in the company that was centralized in family was conditional. Hawthorne Industries was tied up to them and my parents hadn't done anything to separate themselves from their ideals. They'd signed their contracts and pulled us all into a hole right along with them. It was the first thing I was looking forward to doing once the company was in my hands. I'd buy them out and make new contracts.

"Maybe you and Camryn can stop playing games and make it official," Mom said.

I sputtered my water. "Mom. Please."

"If anyone can handle a marriage for convenience, it's her."

"I don't want to think about marriage of any kind."

"It isn't up to you," Dad cut in, dismissing my statement. "You heard your grandfather. If you want the company, you need to do this. End of discussion."

Grandpa stood up, my grandmother followed. She smiled at me, while he took my hand in a firm handshake. "You have five days."

They walked out, Dad said goodbye and walked out after them, and Sam, my mom, and I stayed there with blank stares on our faces.

"I wouldn't be surprised if Camryn or her mother screwed him," Mom said, breaking the silence. "It doesn't matter. He was a lousy lay anyway."

"Jesus Christ," I muttered. "A part of me is glad that you're opening up even though you're two and a half decades late, but can we please not talk about that?"

"You're right." She nodded stiffly and looked away. When she looked at me again, she leveled me with a serious stare. "This is one thing your father and I agree on, you know?"

"I can see that."

"I think it's stupid," Sam said.

"It's what needs to be done," Mom said.

"How are you okay with this?" I asked.

"I just don't understand why that part of the contract can't be changed," Sam argued. "It isn't the nineteen twenties."

"We didn't sign our contract in the twenties," Mom said.

"Still, that was a long time ago. Times have changed," Sam said.

"You're right," she responded. "We have a board of directors now, and they all agreed to those terms."

I scoffed. "A board of directors you should have bought out years ago."

"You knew this was what was expected, Rowan. This isn't news to you."

"I thought you'd change your mind. I don't know. Have a change of heart. Tell the board to go fuck themselves."

"Unfortunately, I can't."

I sat back in my chair, rocking it back on two legs. Mom stood and gathered her purse. She looked at Sam. "I want to get lunch with you before I leave next week."

"Okay."

She looked at me. "With both of you. At the same time. In the same room, eating the same meal, sitting at the same table."

"That's fine, Mom."

"I'll wait for you outside, Rowan." She walked out and shut the door behind her. I groaned, remembering I promised to take her to her favorite little restaurant down the street.

"And then there were two," Sam said. I felt my lip twitch. "I know we don't talk like we used to and we have a lot of shit to get through before we get back to a good place," he said, "but I think you should consider the marriage thing. It can be a fake marriage, just for documents. Hire someone or something."

The thought of marriage made my chest burn. I'd fail at it, and I wasn't the kind of person who accepted failure lightly, but maybe if it was fake . . . maybe.

"Why don't you do it?"

"Because I have no interest in taking over those accounts. Do I want to be a part of it creatively? Fuck yes, but as far as becoming the next CEO, that's your dream, not mine. Besides, dad groomed you for this. It's why they're insisting so much."

"You know how I feel about marriage."

"Same way I do." He shrugged. "Like Dad said, it's a contract. Contracts can be broken."

"I'll think about it." I stood and walked to the door, my steps slowing as I reached it. Regardless of what was happening in my life, I realized one thing: my brother and I were truly in this together. He was getting burned as badly as I was. He didn't deserve to be pushed further into the fire alone. My throat ached as I turned and looked at him. "You want to join us for dinner?"

"What do you think about staying here and raiding dad's liquor cabinet for old time's sake?"

I chuckled. "That actually sounds like a great idea. I'll call Mom and ask her if she wants to bring back food and join us. Kill two birds with one stone."

"Let's do it." He stood up and walked over to dad's office while I made the call.

Two gin and tonics later, we were back to the sore subject of the marriage contract.

"Your father and I were married under similar circumstances. I would've married him without the pretenses, to be honest. I always wanted to marry him," Mom said, lifting her glass of scotch to her lips. My brother and I exhaled simultaneously.

"That doesn't make us feel any better." He reached for the polenta fries between us.

"We had both of you."

"We were a chore," Sam said.

"You were never a chore," she said, placing a hand on her chest as if his words had hurt her.

"Please," I said. "We heard that countless times coming from both of you. You don't have to pretend. It's fine."

"Children put a strain on a marriage," she said. "I loved your father. Still love him. Not that it's ever going to be enough for him."

"You're the reason we never want to get married," Sam said, raising an eyebrow. "Think about that."

"You may find a nice girl and change your mind," she said. I wanted to gouge my eyes out with my fork with all of the marriage talk.

"Fat chance," Sam responded.

"Tessa's a nice girl," Mom said. I reached for some bruschetta and stuffed it in my mouth. Why was I suddenly feeling like I was being ambushed? The memory of my brother kissing Tessa by the pool came flooding back. I tried breathing through it. They were together. They were allowed to kiss. They were allowed to do . . . I couldn't. I reached for my glass, but the words flew out of my mouth before I could even bring the glass to my lips.

"You're not marrying Tessa."

"I never said I was," Sam said.

"But if he wanted to . . . " Mom started.

"Tessa's been through enough because of this family." My voice was hard and non-negotiable, and I could only hope they'd buy into that excuse because I had no idea which other one to provide.

"I'm not going to marry her," Sam said with finality in his voice. I squeezed my glass tighter. Why was this happening and why was I so damn upset over it? I tuned out the rest of their conversation and ate the rest of my meal.

"Your grandparents want us to have nothing to do with the front of the company. They claim that we've made bad business decisions. Them pushing this is their way to try to save the company's image," Mom said, which had me glancing up. I'd missed a lot while tuning them out. My eyes shot to Sam, who looked as if he had no idea what to do when faced with an emotional female.

"Mom, just enjoy dinner," I said. "Let's not talk about Dad or affairs or divorce right now please." I glanced at Sam and mouthed, *Take her drink away.*

It seemed like alcohol only fueled her angry, sad, chaotic state. We sat there, waiting for her to breathe and get her shit together, and I wondered how often she did this in London.

"You're saying this is why one of us needs to get married?" Sam asked. "So that the company can keep its wholesome, family-owned appearance?"

"Yes."

I rolled my eyes. "We live in a world where single CEOs are the norm, both male and female. Anyone can be anything. It's a wonderful time to be alive."

"Not at Hawthorne Fabrics," she said, her voice firm, her eyes narrowed. "We are a family-first company. We are a unit, regardless of what's happening right now."

"We've never really been a unit." I wiped my mouth with my napkin and stood to refill my drink.

"How can you say that?"

"Because it's what we know," Sam said, shrugging. He took a sip of wine and set the glass down. "If anything, you taught us to fend for ourselves. Neither you nor Dad were home most of the time, and when you were, you were hidden behind separate offices, away from us."

"That should have made you closer," she said.

"It tore us apart." I set my utensils down and lifted my glass. "You're right, though, we should have stayed close. We should've figured out how to love and be loved and show support for one another like the Cosby's or the Tanner's or whatever other family show was babysitting us at the time."

"That isn't fair," she said. "We built a great company for you."

"Dad had an affair with his secretary. Had a family with her for God's sake. How could you even talk about family like we ever had one? Was building the company worth tearing down our family?" I needed to get out of there. I hadn't been able to breathe correctly since Tessa's name was mentioned. We went outside and idled by the exit, an awkward silence descending over us.

"I'm sorry that I've been such a failure," Mom said, choking up.

"You aren't a failure, Mom. You dealt with things the only way you knew how," Sam said. I couldn't find it in me to argue with her.

"Yeah, avoidance, and now look, I'm in the middle of a divorce and have two sons who don't even know the first thing about family, and who don't know how to care about others, even each other." She buried her face in her hands, her shoulders trembling slightly.

"I'll take her home," Sam said quietly.

"I'll walk with you."

We walked a block over, where the sidewalk was buzzing with couples and families strolling by. I glanced inside the art gallery when we walked by and wondered who they were showcasing tonight.

"Seems like they've got a full house," I said.

"They're showing Frederick Monte's work today. I guess he started painting while he was overseas and it really stuck with him. Tessa's in there documenting the whole thing for him. He wanted to come, but—"

"Why didn't you go?"

Sam frowned. "We had a meeting."

We did have a meeting, but he didn't have to join us for dinner. He didn't have to offer to take Mom home. He could have excused himself and said he needed to go be with Tessa. She was having a hard time with things. I mean, she blamed herself for her parents selling the company, their divorce, and she was selling the house she loved and grew up in, and now she was acting as a stand-in for her brother? What the fuck?

"It isn't like she asked me to go with her," Sam said. "I'm sure she's fine."

I focused on my steps and putting air into my lungs slowly. Maybe I was reading too much into it. Maybe she didn't want him to accompany her to this. It wasn't like this was her thing, it was Freddie's. I said my goodbyes to them in the parking lot and watched as Sam drove away. The minute his black Mustang disappeared from view, I turned around and headed back to the gallery.

CHAPTER SEVENTEEN

ROWAN

I WALKED INSIDE and smiled at some familiar faces before heading over to the first painting. I stood there for a long time, trying to figure out what the fuck I was looking at. I gave up and looked at the plaque beside it, my eyebrows hiking up at the price. *Jesus, Freddie.* Were people buying this shit? I looked around and saw a couple talking to a man, who I assumed was in charge of sales, and realized they were. I smiled. Good for him. I was still looking around when she walked into the room. My heart stopped beating.

Even if I hadn't known her, I wouldn't have missed her.

Couldn't have. She wore a red dress and flowed into the room like licks of a wild fire, consuming everything in her wake. People turned their heads, conversations quieted. My heart pounded harder, louder, faster. I swallowed to rid myself of the emotion. It wasn't something I should be feeling for my brother's new girl-friend, regardless of who had her first. She deserved to be with someone like him, someone who'd treat her well. I shook the thought out of my head as quickly as it had formed.

No. After all, he wasn't here. And what she deserved was to be free. Being with him would only hold her back, hold her hostage to this town. She flipped her long, dark hair out of her face and turned her head, her gaze clashing with mine. It did nothing to calm my frantic heart. My feet moved toward her. Her lips didn't move, but her eyes smiled as she turned and disap-peared into the next room. She must have known I'd follow, and I did, craving that fire, that burn.

She was looking at one of the paintings, head tilted and lips pursed, when I walked into the room. I wished I could hear the thoughts skipping about in that brain of hers. It didn't surprise me that she chose to walk into the only area in the gallery that was empty. Tessa had always been like that. She sought silence in a room full of people. I loved that about her. Loved that she could be the center of attention in a room and not want it or have a fucking clue she had it at all. As I sidled up beside her, she stiff-ened, as if feeling the charge that lit the air between us.

"What does the queen sprite say about this one?"

She looked up at me, a small smile on her lips. "I like it."

"Just like?"

"Did you bid on it?"

"No."

"Have you bid on any of them?"

"Not yet," I said. "I wouldn't bid on anything without getting the input of a professional art dealer."

She snorted. "You're such a dork."

"You're such a dork," I said, bumping her with my side. She shook her head, smiling as she walked over to the next painting.

"This is one of my favorites."

"It's morbid as fuck." The canvas might as well have been a depiction of the Red Wedding from *Game of Thrones*. I wasn't even sure what I was looking at, but with all the splattered red, that was what came to mind first. Tessa laughed.

"It's a heel," she said.

"I don't see it."

"Like a red-bottom heel." She extended her arm and drew the shape of a heel.

"Why does the floor look like it's covered in blood?"

"Bloody shoes, bloody heels, red bottoms," she said, looking at me as if I were supposed to know this. I didn't, so I tilted my head sideways and looked again.

"Nope. Still don't see it."

"That's one of his more modern pieces. I think he was trying to showcase how much our society focuses on material things and how much they cost us. Let's move on." She shook her head, still smiling as she moved to the next one. We stayed quiet for a moment, staring at the stretch of canvas. It was almost entirely white but had thin black lines that made circles, the way teachers make you practice for better handwriting. She cleared her throat, but her voice still caught and came out a whisper. "This one's mine."

My face whipped to look at her. She looked as if she was about to start crying, but she took a deep breath, and the storm calmed. I looked at the canvas again and at the plaque beside it. *Frederick Monte.* "What do you mean yours?"

"The white canvases with the black lines," she whispered. "I painted those. He told me to sell them, but I said no, so he asked if he could sell them under his name and give me the money."

She shrugged. I looked around the room and realized there were four, maybe five, black and whites. To be honest, they were just scribbles, but wasn't that what abstract art was? Scribbles that made you feel. And hers made me feel pride.

"They're beautiful, Tess." She glanced away to hide her reaction. I moved to stand in front of her and lifted her chin so she'd look at me. I repeated my words, needing her to know that I was seriously impressed. She blushed beautifully and pulled free from my hold. She walked toward the backdoor and pushed it open. Once the door swung shut, my eyes swept the room, and like the fool I was, I followed after her, running down the stairs and walking toward the woods behind the building.

"What happened?"

Tessa shook her head, not facing me. I walked around and stood to block her from fleeing deeper into the forest. I reached out and tipped her chin up again until our eyes met, and hers were welling with tears.

"It's stupid." She blinked, the movement making a tear trickle down her cheek and onto my thumb.

"Tell me."

"I just hate being here without them. I hate selling the house and . . ." She shrugged. I dropped my hand and waited for her to continue. "It's as if nothing matters, you know? Like we're here one minute, and the next, we aren't, and the world just goes on without us. We sold the company, and it's as if no one even remembers our factory was ever there. I drove by the other day, got out, and the guard up front had changed so I couldn't even check out the grounds. It was as if it was never mine. And they're selling Freddie's paintings in there, and he isn't even here to see it. He isn't here to experience the look on people's faces when they finally see his art for the first time. Like it doesn't even matter." She shook her head, laughing a bit. "I told you it was stupid."

"It isn't stupid." I stepped forward and wrapped my arms around her, inhaling against the top of her hair, reveling in her calming lavender scent. I held her tighter. She brought her arms around me, and my heart rocked. If I died right there, in that moment, with her arms around me, I'd die happy. When was the last time I'd felt that sense of comfort? I thought about that for a moment, my mind flipping through memories and coming up short until I pulled up the last time we were together. That was the last time I felt this, and yet, I'd left. I'd broken it off and never looked back. Right then wasn't the time for that either. It wasn't the time to be selfish with her affection, but goddamn, I needed it like I needed my next breath.

"I miss you," she said against me. "I miss your stupid jokes and your stupid laugh and your stupid smile and your stupid bear hugs."

"I'm glad to hear it." A piece of my heart cracked, knowing that I'd missed telling her dumb jokes just to get her to smile and hugging her close like this. I chuckled at her muffled rant, relishing the feel of her against my chest. I wanted to pull back and kiss her, to hike her onto my shoulder and run off with her. The realization rocked me. My heart felt like a ton of weight had suddenly been dropped on it. I'd always wanted her, but I hadn't realized how badly I missed her, just this with her. I reared back and looked at her. "You're with Sam now."

"I'm not." She shook her head, biting her lip as she glanced away briefly.

"You broke up?"

"We were never together."

"It was a hookup?" I almost gagged just asking the words. I didn't want my brother to have had her in ways I hadn't. It was wrong to feel that way, and I knew it. We'd only fooled around, but fooling around with Tessa was the equivalent of a threesome. That was the kind of high I got from her. Maybe it was why we'd never gone all the way together. The thought of giving in so completely had terrified us.

"No," she said. "We were never together—period."

"I saw you kissing by the pool."

She smiled, shaking her head. "Awful timing."

"Your tongue was in his mouth. I don't know how that has anything to do with timing."

"We kissed because we had to, we had to see if we felt anything. Don't you think it would be convenient and easy and just . . . better if I was with someone like Sam? Who didn't drive me crazy? Who didn't make my heart sputter out of control every time he walked into the room? Who didn't make me think insane thoughts at night before bed or make me stay up all night thinking about his lips on mine?"

I closed my eyes and swallowed to keep some semblance of control, but I was losing more and more of it with each second that ticked by. I breathed out, opened my eyes again, and looked at her. "Are you saying you feel that way about me?"

"You know how I feel about you," she whispered.

I wanted to make her say it, but didn't. I didn't need her spreading more of that magic around me, making me go as crazy for her. I had to make sure we both knew this was a bad idea. A horrible idea. I needed to know we both knew it had an expiration date, but of course she knew that. It was me who needed to learn that. I'd once selfishly asked her to follow me to school and it had been a mistake. She didn't deserve to stay here, but damn a part of me wished she would. I felt like a bastard thinking it, but it was true. I needed to stop thinking like that. Last time I'd broken things off because the jealousy would have driven me insane if she'd been mine and I knew she was someplace else, flirting with other guys. It was immature, yes, but I had never claimed otherwise. Having this opportunity with her meant the chance to right my wrongs, and I wasn't sure I was capable of doing that and letting her go again. I swallowed my pride.

"You're leaving for good this time," I said.

"Well, yeah, at least this time we know goodbye is inevitable," she whispered, eyes pleading, mouth parting slightly.

"Because you're only here for another week," I said. She stepped closer, almost flush against me. I tightened my hands at my sides to keep from reaching out just yet, hoping she'd contradict everything I threw at her. Hoping to end this once and for all. We weren't meant to be. We never had been; we never would be. She wanted to be free of this place, and I had ties that rivaled the roots of a white oak keeping me here. I searched her eyes. "Things will never work."

"You're right. It'll end in flames," she responded. My balls tightened. I reached out for her, this time, wrapping an arm around her waist and pulling her against me.

"I hated seeing his lips on yours."

"It meant nothing," she said. "I felt nothing."

"What about now?" I inched closer, heart pounding.

Her eyes shut in a sigh. "You know how I feel."

"I want you to tell me."

"Why? So you can try to mimic my emotions?" She opened her eyes, smiling softly.

My heart tripped. I decided it was best to let her think that. Let her think that I didn't yearn for her the way I did. Let her think I didn't know what love felt like or what it did to a person. After all, it was what I'd said my entire life, wasn't it? I wasn't sure it was far from the truth, and in this moment, I didn't care. I pulled her closer to me and bent to claim her mouth, my tongue delving in and erasing any doubt she may still have about whether I wanted her as badly as I did. I forgot about my responsibilities. Forgot about the pretend wife I was supposed to run and find and practice pretend feelings with. In this moment, my life began and ended on Tessa's lips.

"Let's get out of here," I said, pleased to see she looked as breathless as I felt.

"Please."

CHAPTER EIGHTEEN

TESSA

HE HELD my hand as we walked back to the gallery. It was a simple gesture, but it both warmed and excited me. I couldn't remember the last time I'd held hands with anybody. Surely, in college, but I couldn't remember. It wasn't as if I was living it up anyway. I could count on one hand the number of dates I'd been on. It was a weird time in my life, though. We paused by the door of the gallery. Rowan glanced at me, waiting to see if I wanted to go back in. I simply shook my head, and we continued walking toward the sidewalk. It wasn't that I couldn't go back inside; it was that I didn't *want* to. Maybe it was the way his lips felt on mine or the way he was being so attentive, but I found myself with only one thing on my mind, and that petrified me. Rowan seemed to sense this because, again, he stopped in front of a door, this time one that led to a bar.

"You want to get a drink?"

I looked over my shoulder and scanned the bar. It was loud and rowdy, and I had zero interest in taking part in the chaos. I glanced up at him and shook my head softly. He smiled one of those smiles that warmed me all over, tugged my hand gently, and led me away from the bar. He walked into the grocery store, and I followed with a frown but didn't ask any questions, I simply let him lead me into the wine aisle and then over to the cheese. For a guy who could barely make mac and cheese the last time I spent time with him, he put together a little makeshift picnic pretty damn fast. We paid and walked to his car. I smiled, looking up at him.

"If I didn't know any better, I'd think you had this all planned out."

"Sometimes life hands us lemons, sometimes it hands us grapes." He brought the bottle of red wine up with a grin. "You look like you may need some of the fermented kind."

I laughed a nervous laugh because I wasn't sure where we would go from there. My stomach fluttered with possibilities. We'd messed around plenty of times during our short time together, but it was just that—messing around. We didn't go all the way, and I still to this day couldn't tell you why, but the moment I thought about going all the way with him, I felt like I may die, so maybe that was it all along. Maybe this crazy, intense need I felt for him held me back because I was so afraid of what would happen after. Every time we kissed or fooled around, it had felt as if he took little pieces of me, and I had been afraid that going all the way meant he'd take more than I could handle living without.

Rowan had always driven as if the street was his own personal NASCAR arena, speeding with precision, taking every sharp turn gracefully, and only slowing when we reached residential areas. Tonight, he drove slowly and cautiously, which was a stark contradiction to my rapidly beating heart. He hadn't said where we were going, but when we reached the hill where our parents' houses sat, I assumed it was my big, empty house. Instead, he drove past the houses and over the curb at the end of the road. We bounced around a bit over the gravel as we headed down the hill and stopped by the rocks. Growing up, we'd jokingly call this Lover's Lane.

My pulse skittered. How many times had we met in this exact spot late at night? How many things had we done here during those meetings? I felt my face flame at the memories. It was also where he'd broken things off. Despite all the incredible memories we'd created here, that was the one that glared, stuck its tongue out, and made fun of me for still believing in inconceivable notions with a person clearly unfit to reciprocate them.

I let him lead me down to the shore, hanging back as he laid his jacket down as a makeshift blanket before he extended his hand to me. Only then did my feet move. I took a moment to take off my heels, letting my feet sink into the lukewarm sand as I walked over and sat on his jacket. He sat beside me with a sigh, uncorking the bottle of wine.

"I had forgotten how clear the sky was out here." I buried my hands into the sand behind me and leaned back. It truly was a work of art. One of the paintings that Freddie had put on display was of Orion, not that anyone would know it without my explaining it to them, as messy as it was. "I guess we forget a lot of things when we step out of our comfort zone."

"Or remember them," he said. The bottle popped. The liquid

pouring into the plastic cups followed. "I think that was the thing that surprised me most about being away for so long. I was always surrounded by people, by noise, and I realized how much I missed the silence of this place."

I smiled, sitting upright to look at him as he handed me my cup. "You never appreciated silence."

"I didn't appreciate a lot of things until they were no longer around."

"You can't say things like that, Ro."

"Why not?" He inched closer, tapping his cup to mine.

We held each other's gazes as we took our first sips. What was I supposed to say? That I liked him too much? That he broke my heart when he ended things? I swallowed back all of my emotions and stuck to the safe bet.

"Because it sends mixed signals. I'm either just someone you hook up with, or I'm not."

"You've never been *just* anyone to me. You know that."

"I don't."

"You were my best friend."

I scoffed, turning my attention to the water ahead.

"You were."

"Yeah, well, maybe we should have stayed friends."

He shifted closer, dropping his lips onto my bare shoulder. "Do you really feel that way?"

God, no. He bit my shoulder lightly, and I stifled back a moan. I definitely didn't feel that way. I wanted him with every molecule of my existence despite it all. *Because of it all.* Who even knew anymore? When it came to Rowan, it was as if my brain was stuck in overdrive all the time, not wanting to take breaks out of fear of what it might miss out on. It was dangerous territory, the kind where you knew you needed to hit the brakes and slow down but couldn't because they were malfunctioning.

"We shouldn't do this again," I whispered, meeting his gaze.

His face was close to mine, his lips close to mine. I wanted him to disagree with me. To counter my statement with one of his own.

"I know."

"I'm leaving."

"I know." He leaned in, pressed his lips against mine lightly, and then moved to my cheek, my eyelid.

"I'm not going to let anything stop me from getting out of here," I breathed.

"I would never stop you."

My heart hammered, but when he kissed me again and pressed his hand onto my breast, his fingers stroking slowly, I threw caution to the wind and gave into the temptation.

When we'd come here as teenagers, it was always pitch black out. In the years that had passed, the town had installed lamps every ten feet, and even though we weren't directly beneath any, the soft orange glow of the light bathed us as I straddled him. He unzipped my dress purposely slowly, dragging his fingers down my back along with the zipper. I gasped, arching against him, closing my eyes as my body began to tremble with raw need. He leaned forward, hands cupping my ass, and pressed open-mouthed kisses down my neck.

"Tessa." My name was a groan on his lips as he brought his hands up and unveiled me, discovering that I wasn't wearing a bra. He opened his eyes and met my gaze quickly before cupping my breasts, positioning my pert nipples into his mouth and licking, sucking, nipping. I ground against him again, needing the release the large tent in his pants was sure to bring.

"I've been dreaming about this since your car broke down." He breathed the secret against my chest, bringing his hands between my legs and hooking my underwear aside. The moment he pressed his thumb against my clit, I dug my fingers into his hair and threw my head back with a moan.

"Don't stop," I whispered.

He slid his fingers inside me, his thumb working my clit while his mouth teased my nipples. I felt my core tighten.

"You look so goddamn beautiful when you let yourself be like this," he said, dragging his lips to my throat and finally, pressing them against my own. "I love you like this."

My eyes widened on his, but I kept grinding, kept up the rhythm his fingers had presented me with, faster, matching my rapidly beating heart.

"Please don't stop."

"Never." He brought his face down to my chest again, his fingers increasing the movement between my legs. "I plan on never stopping. I'm going to cherish this body of yours for as long as you let me."

Each word from his mouth brought a new embarrassing sound from my lips that I wished I could control. I was aware of the state we were in—him fully clothed, me almost completely naked, but I couldn't bring myself to care. I was on a rollercoaster and all I could do was brace myself for whatever came next. Everything inside me tightened when his lips fell upon my breasts again. His fingers worked me like strings of a guitar, strumming each chord into something intricate and magical.

"That's it, baby. Let go." He urged, but I was already there.

My heart seized, but my body went thrashing against him, and I screamed his name until I found that place in my mind where no thoughts occurred, only feelings, and that was when I let myself fall.

CHAPTER NINETEEN

TESSA

I WOKE to the sound of my phone vibrating on my dresser. It took me a second, but I opened my eyes, blinking at the light pouring into my room and turning over on my side. Then I remembered. *Rowan.* We'd gotten frisky and tipsy, or at least I had, and he brought me home and stayed the night. We didn't have sex. But we did so many other things that drove me completely crazy. I thought of the way his lips made their way down my naked body and the way he teased me with his tongue until I screamed his name so loud I was sure the entire neighborhood would hear it. I'd returned the favor and once we were spent, we fell asleep, his heavy, muscled arm around me, his lips on my shoulder. I sighed and answered my brother's second phone call in two minutes.

"How'd it go?" he asked.

"The turnout was great." I cleared my throat. "I left toward the end, but there were still a lot of people looking around."

"Colleen called to say seven of the paintings sold."

"Seven?" I sat up straighter. "That's incredible."

"They'll leave them up through the weekend just in case," he said. "Seven is pretty major."

"So major." I smiled wide. "Congrats."

"Thanks. Do you think you'd be able to go by there and sign off on some things on my behalf? Colleen always emails it to me, but it's always much smoother if someone's there to sign off on things. It'll make the process much faster."

"That's fine. When would I have to go in? Today?"

"No, not until they take everything down and start to package."

"Let me know."

"Thanks, Tess."

"Any time."

He paused. "Anything on the house yet?"

"The agent listed it."

"So, it's a waiting game now," he said, exhaling into the line. "Have you decided? New York or Paris?"

"Nope."

"The answer is so obvious to everyone except you."

"Why? Because Mom's over there?" I rolled my eyes. "You know, she doesn't live in Paris."

"Doesn't matter, Tess. You're literally a hop away from the city. Freaking Paris? When will you ever get to say you did that?"

He was right, of course, but still. I loved New York, no matter what anyone said about it. I threw the sheets off and stood on wobbly legs. My muscles were sore. Everything was sore. I smiled.

"Let me know about the papers. I'll be around."

We said our goodbyes, and I tossed my phone onto the bed before grabbing my terry cloth robe on my way to the bathroom. I wondered when Rowan went home. Was he even staying at his parents' old house or did he have his own place? We'd never really gotten around to talking about that . . . or much, really. My face heated at the thought of everything we did. A part of me was disappointed that he left, but I shook the emotion away before it got the better of me. Regardless of what did or didn't happen last night, I had enough on my plate and there wasn't any room for me to worry about Rowan and his feelings or lack thereof. The image of Camryn and her smeared lipstick filled my mind like a dark cloud, threatening to take over my mood. I swatted it away as I stepped into the shower, but all it did was prance around from afar.

After I showered, I threw on my bathing suit, one of my brother's old Air Force t-shirts that I used for the gym, and headed downstairs. In the kitchen, I grabbed a banana and water bottle before going out back. I inhaled the familiar scent of pine and woods as I passed the pool and headed toward the lake. It was sad that I wouldn't have this anymore. Soon, I'd leave it all behind, start my real adult life, and only visit Grandma Joan when I could find the time. With how ridiculously expensive international flights were, if I chose Paris, I wouldn't be able to just hop on a plane and come visit Grandma Joan whenever I wanted.

I neared the end of the forest and nearly tripped over my feet when I saw Rowan standing there, hands on his hips as he looked at the water in front of him as if he were some kind of explorer trying to come up with a name for his new discovery. I stood for a moment, staring at his massive back and the scratch marks I'd left on his shoulders.

"I thought you left."

He turned around, facing me with a smile that made my heart stop for a beat.

Don't be that girl, Tessa. Don't be the woman whose heart stops at the sight of a man just because you've seen each other naked.

I pushed on and closed the distance between us, my heart stuttering when his arm curved around me and his lips came down on mine in a slow, toe-curling kiss. He pulled away slowly and searched my face, eyes twinkling.

"You thought I would leave?"

"I don't know." I shrugged, tearing my gaze from his in hopes to hide my blush, knowing I'd failed at the latter when I heard him chuckle.

"I don't think I've ever seen you blush."

"Shut up."

"Oh my god," he said, voice full of amusement I was not about to partake in. "This is what it takes to embarrass you?"

"Shut up." I groaned, side-stepping him and walking toward his canoe. He laughed harder and wrapped an arm around my middle, pulling my back flush against his chest. His mouth came down to my ear.

"Always running away from me."

"Always chasing me away," I whispered back, heart pounding.

He kissed the top of my head, dropped his arm, and started to walk ahead of me. I tried not to dwell on how bereft I felt without the feel of his touch on me and followed behind. He climbed in, legs slightly apart to balance out the wading of the canoe, and held his hand out to help me step in. He'd placed a white tablecloth on the little seat and a small pillow on either end. There was a basket and two strips of pine needles. I plucked them from the makeshift table, willing my heart to stop racing. He'd put together a picnic for me. For us.

"Those are your flowers," he said. I glanced up at him as a small smile tugged at my lips. "Did I do this right? I can usually tell when you like something, but you aren't saying anything, and you look like you're about to start crying."

"I just wasn't expecting this." I made myself blink rapidly. God. Is this what love felt like? No. I shook the thought away and brought the pine branches up to my nose, smiling at him. "Thank you."

He watched me for a moment and broke the stare before picking up the paddle and taking a seat. I sat across from him and put my hands on my lap, unsure of what to do. Normally, I'd grab a paddle and help, but he only had one in the canoe. I looked over my shoulder and spotted my paddle sitting beside my canoe.

"Should I get my paddle?"

"Nope."

"Should I—"

"Tess." The way he said my name made my attention whip toward him. "I just need you. Nothing else."

My heart jolted, but I managed to keep my mouth shut and not make a fool of myself. *Damn it, Tessa, this is Rowan. Your friend. The guy you used to race on the lake. The one who used to walk you home late at night after parties.* But in all honesty, I could barely remember that time when we'd been just friends.

Maybe because you were always secretly in love with him.

Impossible. What the hell did I know about love anyway? It was just a stupid notion people liked to write poems about. I picked at the pesky thought anyway, like lint on my sleeve. What if I was in love with him?

"You still with me?" he asked, a curious smile on his face.

"Sorry." I blinked and then set the twig of pine on the

cushion and took a deep breath, glancing around. "It's a nice day."

He started to row away from the dock, his back and chest expanding with each wide movement he used to push us along. He'd always been impressive to watch, but today it felt different, as if I were more than just a spectator. If I reached over and touched him, it wouldn't be weird. He grinned, and I snapped my eyes to his quickly, feeling as if I'd been caught doing something salacious. Okay, so maybe it would be weird to lean in and do something. I bit back a smile and glanced away. The water was always serene, but right then, it looked like glass. He stopped rowing near a little floating platform all of us used to visit back in high school. It was kind of our stopping point, or at least mine. If we ever raced, this was the point where we'd go up to. Sam and Rowan used to do it often, and even though Rowan would beat him by a landslide each time, it had always been pretty funny to watch. I looked around and took in the view. It was truly a beautiful day. The sun was shining and the clouds looked like little cotton balls. The perfect painting. I looked over at the houses and spotted his parent's dock. It always stood out because of the amount of canoes and paddles they had laid out. I wondered how much longer it would look like that.

"How much longer will you be living at your parent's house?"

"Not much longer," he said. "The building I'm moving into won't be complete until November, but my apartment should be finished in a few weeks."

"I can't picture you in an apartment with no access to the water."

His lips twitched. "It's on the water."

"Of course it is." I smiled. "What was I thinking, Poseidon?"

He grinned and watched me for a long, silent moment. Long enough that I found myself looking away just to try to ease the tension pulsing between us. "Are we going to talk about last night?"

"We can if you want." I kept my eyes on the horizon, unwilling to meet his gaze just yet.

"Tess." He leaned in, reaching out and pulling my hand to his chest. I swallowed and looked at him. His expression was serious in a way I'd only seen it a handful of times. Normally, he walked around with mischievous eyes, as if he were privy to some joke and the rest of us were the butt of it. I thought about Camryn again and tried not to read into the intensity of his gaze.

"I'm fine, if that's what you're worried about. It isn't like we haven't fooled around before."

"Not like that."

I felt myself blush again. No. Never like that. I hadn't let *any* guy go down on me. I'd always thought it was a weird concept, but with Rowan, things were different, which was part of the problem. He searched my face a second longer before nodding and leaning back a little.

"I have to go to New York this week. You should come with me."

"To New York?" My eyes widened. "I . . . I can't. Not right now with everything going on. Not to mention, hotels are expensive and—"

"I'm not expecting you to pay. And we would be driving, not flying, and as my personal assistant, I think you should come."

"I'm hardly your personal assistant, and you know it."

"You've secured more meetings in a week than the other girls did in months."

"That's because I'm not active on social media."

His lips twisted into a small smile. "I hate that you aren't active on social media."

"Because you can't cyber-stalk me?" My heart dipped at the

way he was looking at my mouth as he nodded. The boat rocked as he moved and braced his arms on either side of me.

"I wouldn't call it stalking."

"What do you call running by my house every morning?"

"Why do you have to label everything?" He leaned in until our noses were touching. My pulse skittered.

"I don't." I swallowed. "Not anymore."

"Good." His lips formed a small, barely there smile as he settled back into his seat. "Come with me."

"I still have to sell the house, and Freddie wants me to sign some papers, and—"

"Everything will still be here when you get back. We'll only be gone four days. They can put a lockbox on the house and leave the papers for you to sign when you get back."

I leaned back, placing both arms on either side of the boat and tossing my head back as I closed my eyes. The sun was hiding behind clouds, which put a damper on my tanning plans, though I knew I'd get some color nonetheless. I jolted when I felt his hand close over my foot. He pulled the other one over the little makeshift table between us, settled them on his legs and started to massage them. A moan escaped my lips unwillingly and my eyes snapped open. His hands were still moving over my feet in a relaxing motion when my eyes met his dark, lust-filled gaze. My stomach flipped.

"Come with me. We'll make a road trip out of it," he said. "I'll need someone who knows about fabric to look at some and to accompany me to an event while I'm there." He squeezed my foot. "Please."

"Fine."

His wolfish grin was the only confirmation I needed to know that I'd made a mistake, but it was too late to go back on my word.

CHAPTER TWENTY

"ARE you sure that's a good idea?" Samson asked, frowning over his beer.

I shrugged. "Is anything I do ever a good idea?"

"Fair point." He shot a pointed look at my whiskey. "If you keep shooting those back you're going to be on your ass before the rest of the crew gets here."

I smiled and took a healthy sip of the whiskey while he rolled his eyes and shook his head, muttering something about not holding my hair back tonight. We had arrived earlier than everyone else, but Rowan promised he'd come, as did Wilmer and Corrigan. Melanie said she'd try, but she was introducing her fiancé to her parents today, so it wasn't likely. I was okay being the only girl in the group because I'd done it so many times, but a familiar female face would have made it better. Plus, I was dying to see her engagement ring.

"How was your meeting with your parents the other night?"

He eyed me warily. "I thought Rowan might have told you since you've been hanging out again."

"He didn't." I frowned. "You guys are talking again?"

"Not really. I mean, not actively, but we're doing better. It's only when your name is brought up that he acts like he wants to kill me."

His scowl made me laugh. "I'm sure he doesn't want to kill you."

"If you can even think that, you don't know my brother as well as you think you do."

"Whatever." I shook my head and took a sip from the almost empty glass of whiskey. "I was kind of having a moment the night of your family meeting, so when we did see each other we didn't talk about him much." Or at all, come to think of it. We were too busy doing other things. I glanced away to hide my blush.

"Because of the exhibition? How'd it go?"

"It went well." I smiled, thinking about it. My smile dropped as I thought about my breakdown. "I feel like things are changing so much, so fast."

I glanced away and caught sight of Rowan walking toward us with Corrigan in tow. My heart picked up the pace at the sight of him. He was wearing a dark T-shirt, which stretched snuggly over his broad chest and shoulders and jeans. I wanted to slide out of the booth and jump on him right there. I looked away quickly, back at Sam, in an effort to control my overactive libido.

"You've never liked change," he said. "You're afraid of it."

I frowned as I let his words settle in. "I'm not afraid of change."

"You are."

"No, I'm not."

"You aren't what?" Rowan asked, sliding into the booth beside me. Corrigan leaned in to give me a kiss on the cheek. Rowan turned to me and pressed his lips to my cheek, the side of my throat, my temple, just like that—bam, bam, bam, the same way my heart beat with his nearness.

"Afraid of change," Sam said, shooting us a surprised look. I'd told him Rowan and I had hung out, but I hadn't mentioned what that meant, mostly because I was still trying to figure it out myself and trying to contain my freak outs to a minimum meant not talking about Rowan and me. I just wanted to, for once in my life, BE and not have things mean more than that. But telling people that meant putting a label on things, and I didn't want that either.

"Nothing," I said at the same time, glaring at Sam.

Cor chuckled. Rowan fought back a grin. I gave them both a look of disbelief. "You agree with him."

"Remember the time they changed our meet location an hour before we were scheduled to be there and you kept banging the steering wheel saying you hated sudden changes?" Cor asked.

"So, because I don't like last-minute surprises I automatically hate change?"

Rowan pulled me close and dropped a kiss on my head. I shrugged him away to look at him, waiting. His lips twisted with amusement, his eyes twinkling. "I'll agree with you if you want me to, but you don't do well with change, babe."

"Don't call me 'babe.' I'm not a pig." I crossed my arms, pursing my lips.

In the past I didn't mind it whenever he'd called me babe. I just didn't want him to call me anything while my blood was sizzling with annoyance. Maybe I didn't like change, but that didn't mean I was afraid of it. Disliking something and being afraid of something were two entirely different things. I said this to them, and the three of them looked like the last thing they wanted to do was argue, but Rowan, of course, couldn't help himself.

"People are afraid of things they don't understand," he said in a calm voice.

I took a healthy gulp of my whiskey. The waiter came by and took Rowan and Corrigan's orders. I let that sink in for a moment. I wanted to argue the point but decided against it. I was all about picking my battles, and it was clear the odds were stacked against me in this case. Rowan ordered me another drink when his came. Sam shot us a warning look.

"How many more can you handle, Tess?"

I flashed him my middle finger. "A lot."

"More than you," Rowan said, putting an arm around my shoulder again. I leaned into him.

"I never said otherwise." Sam's gaze flicked between Rowan and me. "Did you tell Tessa about our family meeting?"

Rowan, who was taking a sip of his drink, started to choke-cough. Somehow, in the midst of the choke-cough, he managed to shoot Sam a look that promised bad things if he continued speaking, which only made me even more curious, though I wouldn't push it right now. Corrigan and I shared a look, and being the great friend Cor was, he stepped in and took the heat off Rowan, who clearly didn't want to talk about their family meeting.

"So, how long are you here for?" he asked me.

"'Till next weekend. You?"

"Same. I got offered an accounting job in Cali. Figured I'd go soak up some rays before I start in a few weeks."

"That's . . . awesome." If I sounded like I was proud of him, it was because I was. Cor hadn't graduated at the top of our class, but because of his rowing skills, he'd landed an athletic scholarship at Columbia alongside Rowan. What he did while he was there was obviously more impressive than the scholarship itself. I smiled because he really had worked his ass off for this opportunity. "I'm proud of you, Cor. You freaking made it."

"I freaking made it." He grinned, bringing his beer to his lips. "Why aren't you tied down yet? It seems like half our senior class is already engaged. You were always the most sought-after girl in school. I thought you'd be the first to get a proposal."

The sip of whiskey I was taking sputtered from my lips. "I think you're confusing me with someone else."

"I'm not." His pale blue eyes twinkled.

"None of you ever showed interest in me," I argued. "I didn't even have a prom date. Rowan had to step up and take me."

At that, both Sam and Corrigan started to howl in laughter. "Poor Rowan, taking one for the team."

I nodded, wide eyed. They both shook their heads, giving me a sympathetic look.

"Why do you think no guys asked you out?" Corrigan asked and then revised, "Aside from the theatre and band geeks."

"I . . ." My brows pulled in. Were they all theatre and band geeks? No. I shook my head. "I had a fling with Billy. He was on the baseball team."

Rowan grunted beside me. Corrigan's eyes danced. I felt so lost.

"What are you not telling me?"

"Billy," Corrigan mused. "Why did he break up with you again?"

"Leave it, Cor," Rowan warned. I glanced over at him and took in his red ears and the way his eyes seemed to shoot daggers. I thought about Billy and why he'd broken things off. I couldn't even remember. Something about focusing on his future and not wanting extra things to stand in the way of the scholarship he was getting. He'd said something about my friends, too, but the memory was muddy at best. I blinked, looking at Rowan and his angry features.

"You warned him away from me."

His gaze slid over to mine. My heart tripped over itself for a beat. I knew girls who'd be flattered by a really hot guy making it difficult for them to date. Some alpha-male move that seemed to drive women crazy, but I wasn't that girl, and Rowan . . . I shook my head. Rowan had made it abundantly clear that he didn't know how to love and wasn't interested in exploring that option, not then, maybe not ever. So why keep me from experiencing it for myself?

"You don't feel even the least bit sorry about that?" I asked, my voice small when it should have been steaming with anger. Anger made me defiant, and I was being far too complacent about this new information.

Rowan simply shrugged. "I'm not much into apologies."

I blinked and blinked again. Took another gulp of my whiskey. I should be upset. Like, really upset. Why wasn't I upset? All those guys in my class never asked me out because . . . and all the while, he was in the middle of on-and-off flings with other girls, Camryn included. My chest started itching as I thought about it. The only answer I could come up with was what I knew to be true in every situation. Rowan was a control freak. Still. That didn't give him the right to control my life. The conversation shifted. Sam and Corrigan were talking about bitcoins and the future of money when Rowan nuzzled his face into my neck.

"Tell me you aren't mad at me."

I pushed him off. "When did you decide you needed to play bodyguard?"

He squeezed his eyes shut. "After I kissed you that night at your grandmother's birthday party."

"You're joking."

"I know. I'm an asshole." When he opened his eyes, he didn't look the least bit sorry.

I never wondered if I was pretty enough or funny enough or anything enough because when I was out with Celia, plenty of guys would hit on me. And I wouldn't trade going to prom with Rowan for the world. We'd had an incredible time dancing and laughing and . . . I thought about my after-prom plans that never came to fruition. Or how I'd actually ended up on top of him in the small confines of his Mustang, only to have him push me away just before things got too hot and heavy. Every other person in our class was planning to hook up that night, and Rowan was, for the first time in his entire life, being the perfect gentleman. I'd heard enough rumors to know he wasn't a gentleman with other girls. Why had he orchestrated the whole don't ask Tessa out thing only to turn me down? He hadn't turn me down that summer, though. That summer, he'd been mine, but only after he decided it. After the countless times he'd tried to fight whatever this was between us and finally claimed me like some Neanderthal claimed his mate, like we were animals with no brains and no free will? So what, no one else could have me because he hadn't deemed it the right time for him to have me? Fuck him.

I excused myself to go to the bathroom. Rowan scooted out of the booth, and I slid out behind him. The music had started already. It was college night, and there were a ton of kids here, little brothers and sisters of our classmates, no doubt. Kids who would leave next week and report to their schools and start their futures. Tonight, they were all dancing sloppily, obviously drunk or high off whatever they had at their pre-game because this bar wouldn't serve minors.

I was sidestepping a couple of girls when I felt a hand on my forearm. I yanked it, not even bothering looking back. Guys were such tools sometimes. I fled into the bathroom and worked on regaining my composure. The past was the past, but with Rowan, it never quite seemed to stay there. Even when I was in college, during the years we didn't speak, I was constantly thinking about him. I lost my virginity to some guy I met at a party, and all throughout, I thought of Rowan. He'd been Christmas mornings and warm summers and a part of him always stayed with me through our years of silence. Stayed with me still. There was a reason I kept a tight lid on those memories and all thoughts of him. It was completely ridiculous for me to even be entertaining this. I had no idea why I had opened myself up to him again even though I knew we'd only break apart again. There were a lot of whys I knew I'd never get answers to because he was him, and he didn't apologize or offer explanations for his actions. He just did.

On that note, I opened the bathroom door again and froze. Rowan was leaning against the wall.

"You're mad at me."

"Nothing to be mad about, right?" I shrugged and walked away from him and onto the dance floor.

He caught my arm. I couldn't tell you what song was playing. All I knew was that our hips started swaying. I gripped his strong biceps as he held on to my waist. We moved, our eyes on each other's, mine angry, his filled with a remorse he'd never speak of.

"You are such an asshole," I slurred, finally. That was how drunk I was. I even knew I was slurring.

"Because I wanted you all to myself?"

"Yes." I reared back, my brows pinching together. "It's like the ultimate double-standard."

My tongue felt heavy, and my words were stumbling all over each other, but I didn't really care. I dropped my hands and stopped moving, no longer feeling the music or the situation. I grabbed his forearms and tried to push his hands off me, but he didn't budge.

"Just let go."

"You'll fall."

My eyes narrowed. "I will never fall."

"Has it occurred to you, Tessa," he said, coming closer, bringing his lips to the shell of my ear, "that you've never actually stood on your own two feet?"

I inhaled sharply and pushed him away once more. This time, he let go. I went outside and walked down the sidewalk, in absolutely no shape to drive. Luckily, I lived close enough that walking didn't bother me. I didn't have to look back to know he was there. I could feel his presence even then.

I hated it.

Hated the way we seemed to be attached by some invisible string. Hated that he knew my next move before I knew my own. Hated that he couldn't fucking admit his feelings or the deeper meaning of why he did the things he did. Most of all, I hated that I wanted him to, needed him to, yearned for him to.

By the time I got to my front door, I was breathing heavily, whether from of my escalating anger or the power walk I just took, I didn't know. I took out my keys and unlocked the door, and just before I shut it behind me, his hand came up to stop it.

"I didn't invite you in."

"I'm not a fucking vampire, Tessa. I can come inside if I want to."

"This isn't your house."

"Soon, it won't be yours either."

"Right." I turned around. "Because you've taken that from me too."

"Oh my god." He looked up at the ceiling with a noisy exhale. "I thought we were past this."

"Says the guy who hasn't had to give anything up. Ever." I crossed my arms. His eyes narrowed.

"You know that isn't true."

"Do I?" I shrugged. "You're taking over the company soon. Isn't that what you've always dreamed of?"

"You know that isn't true," he said again, his tone hard, his eyes searching mine.

Anger continued to burn in my chest like an undying flame. I couldn't seem to put it out or stop myself from pushing him. This morning, I'd woken with a sense of excitement I no longer felt. I was just confused and . . . over it.

"Why didn't you have sex with me on prom night?"

He blinked. "What?"

"I believe you heard me."

He chuckled, an unamused, hard sound that matched the look in his eyes. "Is that what this is about? Sex? You're mad because I talked some loser guys away from you because I was looking out for you and because I stopped you from making a mistake?"

"Oh, you're such a fucking saint," I spat. "Spare me the bullshit. You don't have the right to decide when I make mistakes."

"Jesus Christ." He threw his hands up. "I can't believe we're having this conversation right now."

"Just tell me why. I deserve to know why," I said loudly, and to my absolute dismay, I felt tears swimming in my eyes. I swallowed, brought my voice down twelve notches and whispered, "It isn't like I was going to remain a virgin, you know? I had sex in college with some no one. It was a completely unmemorable experience. But I guess that was what you wanted, right? For everybody after you to be unmemorable?"

"Oh, Tessa." He said my name softly, in a near whisper, as he walked over to me. I wiped my tears away before he got a chance to, but he cupped my face anyway and rubbed his thumbs over my cheeks.

"I'm so mad at you," I whispered.

"I know." He leaned down and kissed my pout, my cheek, my eyelids before pulling back and looking at me. "I'm a selfish bastard, and I'm sorry."

Heart pounding, I reached up and touched his face, brushing his hair back and threading my fingers through it. "You are a selfish bastard."

His large hand felt hot on my back as he pulled me closer. He put his forehead against mine, closed his eyes, and breathed out. I did the same. Our own little *hongi*. We stayed like that for what felt like an eternity, my anger slowly dissipating with each exhale. He pulled away slowly, his hands still on my face as he looked at me.

"You're still coming on the trip, right?"

I nodded. "I told you I would."

He smiled, dropped a chaste kiss on my lips, and headed for the door. "I'll pick you up at eleven."

"You aren't going to stay?"

He shook his head, hand on the door. "If I stay, if . . . if we're going to do this hooking up thing until you leave and then call it a day, maybe we should discuss it. When you're sober."

"I'm sober."

He cocked his head and shot me a look.

"I'm mostly sober."

"Mostly isn't good enough. I'll pick you up tomorrow morning."

"Fine," I grumbled. He chuckled as he walked down the driveway.

CHAPTER TWENTY-ONE

"THAT BOY IS GOING to break your heart again." Grandma Joan crossed her arms as she leaned against the doorframe. She had come over this morning to make sure her friends took everything they purchased, and that everything included my entire childhood bedroom set. I wished she'd leave. I didn't exactly want her here when Rowan arrived, especially since there was no telling what she would end up saying to him.

"I haven't given him my heart to break." My cell phone

charger was the last thing to go into my overnight bag before I zipped it closed.

"Oh, Tess." She sighed heavily. "He's going to keep you here and ruin your chances to become someone."

"That isn't true." I frowned.

Rowan wasn't the type to keep anyone anywhere. As long as I knew that, I'd be fine. Besides, I wanted to leave. I needed to leave. I wanted to argue with grandma, to tell her that I could make a name for myself anywhere, but we'd both know it was bullshit. Unfortunately, location mattered. Grandma Joan shook her head, her thin lips twisted in disappointment. She'd always wanted more for my mom. She wanted her to live her own life, not put it on hold for some man, which Mom did anyway. I could tell she was trying to figure out whether or not she should give me a long speech, but after a beat, she sighed and shook her head.

"Just be careful," she said finally. "Don't get pregnant."

I scowled. "I'm not that stupid."

"Neither was I, and look at how I ended up."

I sighed heavily. I wasn't going to answer that because I knew I'd say something I'd regret. The doorbell rang and cut our conversation short. Mom had that fancy ring on it that used to drive us crazy as teenagers, but as an adult, it brought me comfort. Funny how perception changed over the years.

"I'll be back in a few days. I gave the realtor your number just in case, but he's putting a lockbox on the house," I explained, rolling my bag toward the stairs. I heard her small heels behind me as I picked up the suitcase and walked down with it.

"You'll call," she said. "When you get there. I don't trust that kid's driving."

I laughed. I didn't necessarily trust it either. He drove like a damn maniac. I kept that to myself, though, and opened the door. My heart skipped a beat when I saw him. He was dressed down—joggers and a loose Punisher T-shirt, which somehow didn't manage to hide any of his muscles. My mouth watered just thinking about what was underneath that shirt. I blinked, remembering myself, and he grinned, leaning in to press his forehead against mine and breathe out. My heart skipped another beat, but I managed to breathe out with him. A part of me wondered if he'd taught the *hongi* to another woman. That part of me reared its green head and rooted its heavy feet on my heart. I backed away quickly. That wasn't the kind of emotion a *hongi* was supposed to provide.

Rowan looked at my grandmother, who had a small smile splayed on her lips and a hand on her hip as she waited.

"What? You aren't going to greet me?"

He chuckled, stepping in and doing the same to her. When they stepped away from each other, she tugged his ear hard, making him grunt as she pulled him down to her five-foot-three level.

"You hurt her, I kill you," she said. "How's that for a *hongi*?"

"Nana!"

She shot me a fiery glare that made me cower a bit. Rowan rubbed the tip of his ear with his fingers.

"I promise to keep her safe."

"It isn't her physical safety I'm concerned about," Grandma said, glaring at him.

He simply nodded at this, and I stepped in to pull him away from her before this got any more awkward. He said goodbye and picked up my suitcase, walking outside. I followed and climbed into the passenger seat of his car.

"I'll call you when I get there," I called out with a wave. She waved back, looking non-too-happy with the arrangement.

"She hates me," Rowan said once we drove away.

"Eh." I shrugged.

"The fact that you can't even try to defend that statement means she hates me. That doesn't bother you? You love her."

"Your mom hates me. Does that bother you?"

"She doesn't hate you." He scowled, looking over.

"She hates the idea of us together." I raised an eyebrow, daring him to say otherwise. He looked at the road ahead, which made my heart sink a little. A part of me wanted him to contradict me or at least explain why she hated the idea of me dating him, but I let it be. I would leave soon, and it wouldn't matter.

"She doesn't hate you, though. My mom loves you. Her problem is with me, not you," he responded, but it didn't make me feel even the slightest bit better. "Joan hates me."

"Because she thinks you're a player who will break my heart."

"I'm not."

"I know."

He was a lot of things, but a cheater wasn't one, even if he did seem like one by dating multiple women at once. He was just never the type to settle down, but he always let it be known to all parties.

Except you. He was with her. And he was with you.

The thoughts snapped at me like a barracuda. Snap, snap, snap. The way I wanted to snap, snap, snap her neck every time I saw her. I pushed it away. He hadn't been with anyone else while we were together. I knew that without a shadow of a doubt.

"I would never purposely hurt you," he said, reaching over and sliding his hand over mine. I closed my eyes for a moment and breathed, enjoying the moment.

"I know that."

"Did you RSVP for the cocktail thing?"

"Yes. It starts at five thirty, but the hotel I booked is right by it, so it shouldn't be a problem."

"We'll be there by four," he said. "Is that enough time for you to get ready?"

"Uh, yeah, is it enough time for you to style your hair?"

He winked. "Guess we'll find out."

I smiled, shaking my head and glancing away to hide my blush. "It's going to be miserably hot this week."

"Is that why you're wearing that flimsy little sun dress?"

"Yeah." I smiled, glancing over at him. "I'm glad you took note of the kind of fabric I'm wearing."

"No comment."

"What does that mean?" I looked down at my sundress and frowned.

It was a super cute, albeit, flimsy little dress I'd purchased during the Free People super sale a few months back. Like most of their clothing, it was whimsical and, yes, a tad revealing, with spaghetti straps that showed off my entire back. I'd covered myself with a jean vest, so he hadn't even caught a glimpse of that part. Not that I wasn't showing enough skin to begin with. The low neckline exposed the tops of my breasts, and I was pretty sure he could see through most of the material past the bodice, which was why I'd worn ivory panties. I looked up at him, still frowning.

"Why no comment?"

"Because if you knew how hard I've been since the moment I picked you up, you wouldn't be as amused about my noticing the fabric." His words shot straight between my legs. I shifted a little in the seat.

"Oh."

"Yes, oh."

I bit my lip, eying the tent in his joggers. I could definitely see it, huge and hard and ready. It made me clench my legs together again. It took every ounce of self-control I had not to reach over and free him.

"You're driving. You need to focus on that."

He sighed. "You're right."

His response made me wonder how many times women had gone down on him or jerked him off while he was driving this car, and just like that, I went from turned on to bothered. I folded my arms in front of my chest again and looked out the window.

"What's going on up there?" He reached over and tucked my hair behind my ear, giving him a clear view of my face.

"I'm trying *not* to think about how many women have done dirty things to you in this car."

He chuckled, shaking his head as he focused on the road ahead. After a moment, it was clear he wasn't going to answer me, which further pissed me off.

"Have there been that many?"

"I'm not having this conversation with you."

"Why not? We're friends again, aren't we?"

"Friends?" He shot me a look. "Is that what we are?"

"You were the one who fled the scene yesterday and said we were going to discuss things."

"I did, didn't I?"

"So? Shall we discuss?" I turned to face him. "Why are we discussing this anyway? Don't regular people just hook up and break it off when it's over?"

"We aren't regular people."

"Okay. Do you discuss this with all the women you hook up with?"

"Not necessarily, but you aren't like them."

"Because what? You think I'll fall in love with you? Or is this about the stupid change thing that I'm supposedly not good with?"

"Taking you to Lover's Lane the other night wasn't the smartest thing to do." He sighed. "I just want to be clear on things because you're leaving, I'm not, and . . . well, we need boundaries."

"We never needed them before. We went our separate ways when you ended things."

He stayed silent for a beat. "You know what, let's talk about that, since you're so keen on arguing these days."

"I'm not keen on arguing. I just think you're full of shit."

"Remember when I asked you to go to Columbia with me and you chose Yale?"

I rolled my eyes. "Big whoop. Your girlfriend chose Columbia. I thought you'd be satisfied with that."

"She . . ." He shook his head. "She isn't my girlfriend. Never was."

"Not what I heard."

"Enlighten me then."

"Did you forget about Facebook? If they had been giving out medals for the most posts made in a day, Camryn would have won. And guess who was in ninety percent of them?" I shot him a look. He breathed out noisily through his nose.

"Not my doing. I didn't ask Camryn to follow me to college. She decided to take it upon herself to wedge herself further into my life by posing as my girlfriend in some circles and *soon-to-be* girlfriend in others, I knocked the rumor down until I was blue in the face. Still, it hadn't mattered with some of the girls at school."

"I bet you didn't try all that hard." I shrugged. "Doesn't matter. We'd already broken up."

"Because you chose Yale."

"That is not why we broke up and you know it. Besides, I chose to follow my dreams, Rowan. How can you, of all people, fault me for that? Or are you jealous that I had the balls to do something you didn't?"

He stayed quiet. I sighed. Why was I upset again? I turned the radio up and started scrolling through stations. Rowan and I had a difference of opinion on most things, including music, so we normally kept the radio off, but bickering about songs was better than bickering about him having sex with other women or why I followed my dreams instead of his.

Though, him rubbing in the fact that I didn't follow his lead and that we didn't stay together because of it pissed me off. What kind of power did he think he held over me? Maybe that was the problem. He was so stuck on his own ego and the way people walked around on eggshells around him that he didn't even realize some of us had our own thoughts.

"It's a touch screen," he said. "You don't have to stab it."

"I'm not stabbing it." I jabbed the screen once more and stopped at the Nineties pop station, catching the tail end of an N'SYNC song I knew for a fact Rowan hated. Then Avril Lavigne started to sing, and instead of changing the station like I normally would have, I turned it up, knowing it would irritate the crap out of him. I expected him to try to turn it, or at the very least mock the lyrics, but he started to sing. Loudly. His eyes smiling as he looked over at me and caught the surprised look on my face as he started to sing about making things complicated.

Oh god. I covered my face. He had an awful, terrible singing voice. Despite myself, I started to laugh, and laugh, and laugh. And finally, I uncovered my face and joined in on the impromptu car karaoke moment, singing the next chorus with him. Never in a million years would I have thought he'd know the lyrics, but then Rowan was always surprising me one way or another. We sang loudly, stealing glances as he drove down the freeway, and by the end of the song, I had tears in my eyes because I was laughing so hard.

"You're an awful singer," I said between laughs. "Like, awful."

"You aren't so great either."

I shook my head, smiling so widely my cheeks hurt. "I thought you hated that song."

"I do." He chuckled. "How do you think I know it so well?"

"Because Roger loved it," I offered, laughing even harder as I thought about his old rowing teammate who was obsessed with anything nineties and everything Beyoncé. He joined in, shoulders shaking. "How is he anyway? Do you keep in touch?"

"He's fine. He invited me to his wedding next summer. I'm supposed to be in the party."

"Oh?" My brows rose. "I'm assuming he's marrying a man."

"You would be right." He grinned. "Nice guy too. Accountant."

"Roger with an accountant? Geez. Opposites really do attract. What is he doing with his life?"

"He went to culinary school and got on full-time at a good restaurant in New York."

"Nice. Good for him." I smiled. Rowan put his hand over mine on my lap again.

"I don't want to hurt you," he said after a moment. "The last thing on Earth I would ever want to do is hurt you."

"I know." I squeezed his hand. "I'm sorry about what I said."

"Don't be." He grinned. "You're right. I am a little jealous of you. My entire life I wanted to be a college professor, but I've always known my place in the world, and it resides in Hawthorne Industries. I've come to terms with that."

"You know that you could do both."

He shook his head. "You know how I am."

"Balls to the wall."

He chuckled. "Pretty much."

"Well, for what it's worth, I think it's commendable."

"I don't regret what we did the other night," he said. "A part of me wishes I could be strong enough to stop myself, but I just . . . when it comes to you . . ."

"I know."

"You leave soon, and I don't want to go back to being strangers."

"That was your doing," I said, though I wasn't sure if I had it in me to stay friends once I left. Would that entail seeing him with other women and vice versa? I wasn't sure either one of us were built to handle that.

"I know. I fucked up. I don't want to fuck up again. I'm just putting it out there."

"Is this your way of telling me that if I try to have sex with you, you'll turn me away?"

"This is my way of telling you I won't turn you away, and I'm not sure how I feel about that."

I wasn't sure how I felt about it either. Excited, anxious, terrified. At least I knew I wasn't alone in this.

CHAPTER TWENTY-TWO

ROWAN

I GLANCED around the cocktail party, looking for Tessa. She'd told me she'd meet me down here once she finished getting ready. I was talking to a man who owned a factory down in Queens about where he imports his fabrics when I finally spotted her. She was wearing a tight black dress that hit her knees and red lipstick. Her brown hair cascaded down in soft waves that people paid big money to achieve and she had naturally. She laughed at whatever the man she was talking to was saying, and I felt it in my groin. I wanted to take her away from here and have my way with her, the way I'd been dreaming about for over ten years.

Tessa had no idea the kinds of things she did to people. I watched the way she managed to wrap every man in the room around her little pinky as she spoke to them. It was her smile. It was the way she acted as if she was held captive by your words, regardless of what you were saying. She had a way about her that put people at ease and made them talk. Two qualities I needed in order to take this company to the next level. Two qualities my fake wife should definitely have. I only had a few days left to decide. I'd spent most of my time trying to figure out how to get out of it, but the more time passed, the more unlikely it seemed and I knew thinking about Tessa being the woman signing that contract was stupid. She wouldn't go for that. Hell, she wouldn't even follow me to college. I wasn't stupid enough to believe she'd marry me out of convenience. A man could dream, though.

"These are the newest fabrics we got from Peru. They're even more vivid in person," Mr. Ferrero said. I made myself look at his phone screen and then took it from his hand. Damn. The fabric was nice.

"You have this in Queens?"

"I have samples of most of it. I just brought back a shipment of the red one and this ivory."

I let him scroll and show me the ivory.

"Can I show this to my assistant?"

"Sure." He smiled, allowing me to lead him over to where Tessa was standing.

She looked up, her gaze finding mine before we reached her. I felt a sense of . . . something tickling my chest when she looked at me like that. If I were being completely, no-bullshit honest, Tessa was the only woman who could look at me and send my heart into a frenzy. I pushed the thought away. It was nostalgia. That was why I felt this way. She introduced me to the man she'd been speaking to—Cody, a buyer for Barneys, and I introduced her to

Mr. Ferrero. After a moment, Cody excused himself to speak to someone else and I asked Mr. Ferrero to show her the fabrics.

Tessa gasped, taking the phone from his hand when she saw a couple. She glanced up at him with a shy smile. "I'm sorry. Fabric is my jam."

He smiled widely. I was sure he was excited to have such a gorgeous woman paying attention to his products and launched into the same speech he just gave me about his suppliers.

"The Vietnamese one looks lovely," Tessa said in awe. "Do you sell to a lot of cloth manufacturers or do you manufacture in-house?"

"We do most of the work in-house unless the purchasing company has their own factory. Normally, the big brands buy the fabric and go elsewhere to make their product."

"My father used to own a fabric company, and for years the biggest client was the government, but our name wasn't on any of the final products."

"It's like that for us." Mr. Ferrero smiled, scrolling to the next picture—the ivory fabric. "This is for a well-known dress maker. We make some of the dresses in house for them, but you'd never know it."

"Oh my god. I would kill to feel this fabric." She looked up at him. "Do you have lace? Do you only sell wholesale? Is it all in Queens?"

I chuckled. Mr. Ferrero gave a belly laugh that made Tessa smile brightly. Damn, I wanted to kiss her again.

"I can make an exception for you. What do you want it for?"

She took a breath and explained to him that she designs wedding dresses, and even though she wasn't planning on sewing them, she'd like to start collecting swatches from different places just in case. As she spoke, I could feel her passion, her brown eyes lit with every sentence, her voice got a little higher, a lot faster, and she looked absolutely beautiful. By the end of it, she even had me convinced that I wanted to start dressmaking, and I didn't know the first thing about it. I thought about the folded piece of paper, the discarded design, that I had in my wallet. Was that the dress she was thinking about when she looked at this fabric? I wondered how often she thought about her own wedding dress, if at all. She shot me a look that said *hello, earth to Rowan*, and I blinked rapidly.

"I'm sorry. What was that?"

"I was just telling Mr. Ferrero what an incredible company Hawthorne is and that it might be good to go to Queens to see if you could buy any of his fabrics."

"Oh." I nodded. "That's an excellent idea. We can talk pricing and volume."

"And I can give Tessa the inside scoop on the fabric I'm getting from Colombia next month."

I smiled because it was what was expected, but the thought of next month made me feel uneasy. She'd be gone next month.

Unless you convince her otherwise.

My wallet pinched my backside, reminding me of the dress. Wedding bells rang out. I took a sip of the wine I'd been holding and pushed the phantom sound away. I let my gaze linger on hers when I excused myself to talk to different people and she smiled, wordlessly telling me she'd keep going around the room. I wasn't sure how, but I managed to yank myself away from her and walk around the room to network, but all the while, I was thinking about getting right back to her. In short, I was in deep shit.

CHAPTER TWENTY-THREE

ROWAN

Past

IT WAS hard to concentrate on what Camryn's dad was saying when I had to fight off his daughter's hand on my leg every five minutes. It didn't matter how many times I'd made it clear that I wasn't interested in her like that, it was as if she didn't hear my words clearly. Or maybe it was rejection that she didn't know how to handle.

The last place in the world I wanted to be was at the dinner table with all of them, but Dad had told me earlier this week that

I needed to be there, that it wouldn't look right if Sam and I didn't show. Yeah, well, if that were the case, where was Samson? He seemed to get away with everything—not being present at dinners like this, not having to go into the office with Dad, not attending meetings, and picking and choosing what gala he wanted to go to instead of having to go to them all. Most of the time, I didn't care. The oldest son was the one with all the responsibility, after all, but this one got to me because I knew he was over at Freddie's house while I was stuck, waiting for the time to tick by. Sunday nights were pizza night at the Monte house, and a group of us always went over. I pushed Camryn's hand away – again – and shot her a look. She smiled saucily, batting her eyelashes at me like I was going to fall for it.

If that hadn't been enough, her mother was looking at me weird, in that way the women at the grocery store looked at me nowadays. Sam said it was happening more and more to him as well. At least he still had a year left. For me, it was as though turning eighteen had put a stamp on my forehead that said, "Hey, I'm not exactly jailbait anymore."

"Why don't you take Camryn over to Tessa's tonight?" Dad asked. "Isn't that where you kids disappear to on Sundays?"

Camryn yanked her hand from my lap and sat upright beside me. "That's okay. I'd rather just stay in."

"I promised the guys I'd go over there after dinner. You can stay here and watch a movie if you'd like," I said. I didn't have to look at Camryn to know she was brooding. She probably wanted to stay in because it was better than seeing Tessa and I together. Not that we were official or anything, but we were definitely more official than I'd made any of the other girls I'd dated. I held hands with her, I took her out to dinner and movies, we hung out and talked. We weren't just about fooling around or having sex. I hadn't had that before. Not like this anyway.

After a long, silent moment, Camryn sighed and said, "I'll

just go. There's probably nothing interesting on television anyway."

"We'll pick you up there when we're ready to go," her mom said with a smile.

Normally, I took an ATV over there, but she didn't need another excuse to have her hands all over me, so I opted for Dad's golf cart.

"Is Wilmer going to be there?" she asked as I drove.

"Maybe."

She sighed. "He's the only friend you have that I can stand."

Translation: he was the only friend I had whose trust fund exceeded mine and Sam's. I hoped he would be there. At least it would take her attention away from me for a while. We parked and walked up the steps to the door, all the while Camryn commenting on how quaint their house was. I'd never really noticed. But over the last year or two, this house had started to feel more like home than my own did. I knocked and waited. Celia opened the door, her wide smile completely vanishing when she saw Camryn. She greeted us nonetheless.

"I hate these bitches," Camryn muttered under her breath as we followed her in. "They have nothing, yet somehow, they think they're better than me."

I kept my mouth shut and kept walking, knowing that responding would make Celia turn around and probably punch her, which would lead to a lawsuit, no doubt. Camryn's parents were about that lawsuit life. Her mother had pressed charges on a pregnant woman who accidentally let her grocery cart go and scratch her car in the parking lot. I spotted Sam and Tessa beside him, looking up at him and laughing as he told a joke. I envied my brother so much, but never more than in those moments, when he was with her while I'd been tied down to doing something I didn't want anything to do with.

Lately, it seemed like most women were paying a little more

attention to me, and then there was this girl who lived up the block with the naturally tan skin and almond-shaped eyes, who I knew wouldn't have even given me a second glance if she didn't know me. It was weird that I noticed it, all these years later. Weird that she was so quick to call me on my bullshit when everyone else stayed quiet. Weird that I was vying for one girl's attention when I had it coming at me from all corners. It was hard to explain, but that was how it was. It was like a color splash effect on a black-and-white print, everything muted except for Tessa, with her wavy locks and bright smile. And there she was, turning all that magic to Samson.

I felt a hand on my arm and remembered Camryn. Fucking Camryn. I exhaled and said hi to a few of the guys before making my way over to my brother. I said hi to Freddie first. He'd just come back from a three-month boot camp and was waiting to hear where he'd be sent next. By the time he finished telling me about drills and sergeants, I looked up and noticed Tessa was no longer sitting by Sam.

"Missed you at dinner," I said.

"I'm sure you did." My brother smirked. "Mom made you bring the princess along?"

I looked over to where Camryn was flirting with Wilmer, looked back at my brother, and cocked my head in a what-do-you-think motion. He shook his head, his lips twisted in distaste, but he didn't say anything. I looked around the room. There were more people here than usual and a lot of unfamiliar faces, mostly guys.

"Who are all these people?"

"Freddie's Air Force buddies."

I gave a nod, scanning the room for Tessa and finding her talking to two guys I'd never seen before. She said something they both laughed at, looking equally as interested in tearing off a piece of her. I scowled and looked around for Freddie. Was he not seeing this? Not that he'd ever interfered with her past boyfriends, and thankfully, he didn't interfere with me either, but they'd been nothing like these two. The two talking to her were men, and even though I was bigger than one of them, they both had that soldier thing about them that made them look badass. I chalked it up to the tattoos. I stopped by the kitchen, grabbed a cold Stella and made my way over there, catching the tail end of a conversation. One of them was inviting Tessa to visit him in Chicago, and she was being wishy washy about the invitation, the way someone did when they knew they weren't going to go through with something but didn't want to be rude about it. I wished she'd say flat-out no, but I couldn't demand such a thing, especially since it was my idea for us not to be too serious.

She was still smiling when she glanced over and saw me walking over. Her eyes widened slightly, but her smile stayed intact. My heart did a little gallop.

I do not bleed. I do not feel stupid emotions that won't propel me in life.

I thought of my dad's mantra and tried to stick to it, but when I reached her and she wrapped an arm around me in a sideways hug and I inhaled her scent, I forgot about responsibilities and mantras and military guys with tattoos. I only saw Tessa. She introduced me to the guys—Dante and Billy. We made small talk for a bit. They'd joined when Freddie joined and went to the same boot camp. Like Freddie, they were waiting for their call and would more than likely be overseas by Christmas. I asked them what I asked every soldier I'd ever met thus far.

"Why'd you enlist?"

One said he wanted to serve his country, while the other told me he hadn't gotten into college and didn't know what he wanted to do with his life, so he went with this.

"Both my grandfathers are veterans," I said. "I never felt

inclined to join. My brother thought about it a few times, but I don't think he will either."

"Who's your brother?" One of them, Billy, asked.

"The one with the Mets cap." I pointed over.

They gave a nod and turned back to me.

"You play football?"

I shook my head. That was the first thing people thought when they looked at me. "I row."

"Rower," one said nodding. "Sure you don't want to enlist?"

I laughed. "Pretty sure, but don't count me out just yet."

We small talked a little longer before I walked away and followed Tessa, who was refilling the beer cooler. Her eyes snapped up when she felt someone walking near.

"You brought Camryn."

"She was in my house."

She rolled her eyes. "Of course she was."

"What's that supposed to mean?" I tossed my beer into the recycling and picked up another. Tessa got her own, shook her head, and walked out the back door. I followed. "Tess, I'm confused."

"Confused about what?" She stopped and faced me. "You know she hates me, yet, you bring her over. For what? So she can disrespect me in my house?"

"She doesn't hate you." I flinched at the face she shot me before walking farther into the forest. "She won't disrespect you. I won't let her. I didn't have much of a choice."

She stopped and turned around again. "You always have a choice."

"Not with this."

"You say that about everything when it comes to her. Let me guess, she doesn't give you a choice every time she sticks her tongue down your throat either?"

I searched her face, heart hammering. She was jealous. This

girl that normally acted like she didn't give a shit about who I hooked up with in the past, was actually jealous. Did it make me an asshole to feel this excited over it? To think maybe this affected her the way it did me? When I wasn't around her the only thing I thought about was being around her. At night, I lay awake thinking about her lips, the mischievous look in her eyes, her small hands on me, and I stroked myself using every one of those images. I stepped closer, completely up in her space. Her eyes widened a little. Her mouth parted slightly.

"People can see us, Ro," she whispered, and even that made me hard. I brought my hand up and brushed her hair back, cupped her chin.

"So what, Sprite?"

She laughed lightly. "Why do you insist on calling me that? My ears are *not* that pointy."

"Because you weave some serious magic." I put my other arm around her, letting my beer hang a little as I walked her deeper into the trees, pushing her against a bark. "The kind that makes a guy forget his name."

"You've never forgotten your name around me."

"You don't know that."

"I've known you too long for your lies to work on me." She tilted her chin up, and I leaned in, bringing my lips down to her exposed neck. She moaned, bringing a hand up to my hair and tugging, my name a delicious gasp from her lips, "Rowan."

God. What I would do to hear her say that over and over again. My lips didn't stop, couldn't stop moving against her neck, her jaw, her cheeks, her eyelids, her forehead, her nose. I stopped just before I reached her lips, pulled back slightly to look into her eyes so that she'd know that this would change things. People seeing us like this would make us more official than we'd initially intended on being, mostly because both of us were scared of the consequences, of the heartache that this may lead to. There was something about putting this out in the open that intensified that fear. I needed her to be okay with that. Instead of answering, she pulled my lips to hers and kissed me. It was soft and tentative at first as we reacquainted our mouths, and soon, the kiss turned hot and frenzied, all teeth and tongue and growls. I knew that night that there was a slim chance things would end well between us. I knew I needed to stick to the boundaries I'd set for myself with her, because crossing lines with Tessa would be disastrous. She had the kind of magic that turned me inside out. The kind that would make me believe that maybe I did bleed.

CHAPTER TWENTY-FOUR

TESSA

Present

WE WENT out to dinner after the cocktail party. Rowan was starving, and I wasn't quite ready to go back to our shared hotel room. Shared. I still couldn't believe I'd agreed to that, but there was no taking it back. It wasn't as if we hadn't slept in the same bed together, but it was literally all we'd ever done on a bed—slept. Since we'd discussed hooking up and going all the way, the energy around us had changed. It was as if the entire time as we networked at the cocktail party, each stolen glance, small smile, brush of hands as we passed, was a dance of foreplay. The realization made my feelings tangle. I hadn't realized that I could feel this way about him this quickly, but here I was, feeling like every nerve inside me was alight whenever he turned those blue eyes my way. I knew I needed walk the line carefully, though.

The last time we had a limited amount of time together, he'd hurt me like we'd been together for years. Maybe it was because, in my mind, we had been in some weird, twisted way. I tried to shake the thought away. We were more mature than we had been. We both knew exactly where our lives were supposed to be headed. It wouldn't be like the last time.

"You haven't said much since we left the party," he said, making the ice in his whiskey glass tumble with the movement of his wrist. I did the same to mine and took a sip.

"Neither have you."

He gave a nod. "I love watching you in your element."

"It's your element too." I tried and failed to fight the blush on my face. What was it about him saying nice things to me that set my skin ablaze?

"Not really. I do it because I have to, you do it because you love it."

"You keep saying things like that." I set my glass down. "You can do anything you want. Why let yourself be tied down to this?"

"You know why."

"Yeah, but you've never brought it up this much before, so obviously, it's on your mind and bothering you."

He sighed, running a hand through his soft hair. "It's what's been expected of me since I was born, and things just got a hell of a lot more complicated for me."

"Because of the divorce."

"That's part of it." He looked as if he wanted to say more, and his eyes were suddenly even more intent on mine in a way that made my stomach flip. "Where do you see yourself in five years?"

I laughed awkwardly, not really expecting that. I picked up my glass again and took another sip of the whiskey. "That's such a high school year book question."

"Hey, we both got friendliest in the superlatives, didn't we?"

"We did."

"And most good-looking."

I felt myself smile wider. "We did."

"And king and queen."

"Yep."

"And most driven."

My cheeks hurt from smiling. "Where are you getting at with this?"

"Maybe our fellow classmates were on to something."

"Meaning?"

"Meaning maybe we're perfect for each other. Always were."

My smile dropped shakily. I thought the point was not to get attached. Why was he bringing this up? "Do you believe that?"

"I do."

"So why did we have a conversation about being careful and all that jazz?"

"Because you're leaving and a relationship would be impossible to maintain."

I swallowed. "Where does Camryn fit into all of this?"

"Why do you keep bringing her up?" His brows pulled together as if he were trying to figure out a confusing equation.

"Because just the other day, she walked out of your office with lipstick smeared all over her face." He exhaled heavily, dragging his hand through his hair again. I waited. When he didn't respond, I continued, "I know you think she and I have some sort of competition for your affection, but I want no part of it. I'm not a teenager anymore. I know my worth and—"

"Tessa." His tone and the way he leaned in made me shut my mouth. "When it comes to you, there's never any competition. You blow everyone else out of the water."

"So why do I feel like I'm always in last place with you? Like I'm always left wading in the water while everyone else has a place on your blue canoe?"

His brows rose in surprise. "You really feel that way?"

"I wouldn't say it if I didn't."

He gave a humorless laugh and shook his head. "And here I was thinking I was chasing after you all along."

"Look." I set my glass down again. "I agree with you on this— I'm leaving in a few days. I don't want a relationship. I'm not looking to settle down with you and start a family. Not that you'd want that anyway." I shot him a look. He simply stared. Waiting. "I just don't want to feel like the other woman in this. I don't want to do more with you and feel like you're cheating on her with me, and saying you and I are perfect for each other . . . well, that's just confusing."

"You would never be the other woman," he said. "You don't believe in love, you don't want to get married, you just want to hook up. I don't believe in love, marriage, and I just want to hook up. That equation equals perfect. As far as Camryn goes, did she try to hook up with me the other day? Yes. Did she kiss me in my office? Yes. Did I entertain it? Fuck no. Why would I do that knowing you would be there?"

"Because you saw me kiss your brother and you wanted payback."

He flushed and looked away. I rolled my eyes. Typical Rowan. He did want payback, whether he planned it or not. "You're so childish sometimes."

"I'll own that accusation." He looked into my eyes again before reaching over and caressing the top of my left hand. My heart wiggled. "I'm a jealous bastard when it comes to you. You know that."

My heart dipped. When he talked about shooing guys away, he'd said he was a selfish bastard, not a jealous one. "I wasn't aware you were capable of feeling jealous."

He shot me a look. I smiled. We asked for the bill and walked hand in hand back to the hotel. As we went up the elevator, I felt like I might just die right there. There was absolutely no coy way of starting this. It surprised me that I even felt this worked up about it, being that we'd been to this rodeo. Sure, this time it would be more. But there was no other reason for two people this sexually attracted to each other to share a bed. I felt his breath on my neck as I shakily unlocked the door, his lips on the slope of my shoulder, where he dropped an openmouthed kiss. My eyes slammed shut, my heart pitter-pattered with raw excitement and need.

I pushed the door open and stepped inside, he shut it behind us and turned me around, pinning me against it as his lips came down onto mine. His mouth was a jolt of excitement, but the kiss was softer than I expected. His lips moved with the sensuality of a lost lover, the feel of his tongue stroking mine in a soft caress, his fingers threading into the hair at the nape of my neck, tilting my face, seeking more. I dropped my key, my purse, and wrapped my arms around his neck, molding against him, needing to erase the inches of space between us. When he broke the kiss, just as slowly as he had started it, our lips took their time parting ways.

"You're sure about this," he said.

"Positive."

"If you ever want to stop—"

I pulled him into another kiss. He nibbled on my bottom lip, I returned the favor, and when our faces were inches from each other's again, I looked into his dark, lust-filled gaze and felt my stomach sinking farther to its knees.

"I want you on our bed," he breathed. *Our bed.*

I took his hand and led him to the room. When I turned around to face him, my breath caught at the wolfish, sensual smile on his face. His gaze lingered over me, traveling down my body in a slow caress that burned every inch it explored.

"Do something," I whispered.

"I fully intend to." He lifted his gaze to meet mine as he closed the distance between us and dipped his face. His mouth touched my forehead as he brought his hands behind me and unzipped my dress. I shrug my arms out of it and let him tug it past my hips so that it fell and pooled at my feet. "You look stunning tonight, by the way," he said, the husk in his voice making the butterflies in my stomach summersault.

He caught my gratitude in his mouth as his lips came down on mine. With deft fingers, he unhooked my bra and pulled it away from me as I stepped out of the dress and walked with him toward the bed, lowering my hands to the buttons of his shirt and undoing one with each step, my eyes on the task as he watched me. When I pulled his shirt open and reveal his taut, muscular, tan stomach, I paused for a beat and then leaned in and placed a kiss on the center of his chest, licked the perfectly dented line between his pecks. He sucked in a sharp breath as I licked my way down, his hands coming up to either one of my shoulders. For a moment, I thought he was going to pull me up again, but he left his hands there as I made my way to the elastic of his boxers.

My name was a broken whisper from his lips. I glanced up through my lashes and caught his lustful stare as I pulled down his boxers. He kicked away his clothes, threw his shirt to the floor, and put his hands on my head. I pressed kisses up and down his shaft, ran my tongue over it, and added my hand into the mix. His breathing became labored, his fingers tightened in my hair. I opened my mouth and swirled my tongue around the tip, loving the way he pulsed and got harder. I stroked him and sucked in a synchronized motion, slowly at first, then faster, then slowing down again. He groaned and groaned and pulled my hair, panting my name.

"My turn," he grit out on a restrained breath.

I shook my head, sucking again. He tightened his fingers even more, pulling me away so that his cock was no longer within my mouth's reach. With his hand on my neck, he slowly pulled me up to stand and leaned down to capture my mouth with his, his tongue diving in with force, swirling around mine and amplifying my arousal. My fingers dug into his biceps. He pushed me away and settled into the center of the bed, his hard, veined cock springing up between his muscled legs and perfect six-pack. He was perfection. I settle between his legs, which were hanging from the bed, and began to climb over him, stopping just before our centers met. He shook his head, eyes hot on mine.

"Come sit on my face."

I felt his words in my core and hesitated, unsure if I could even last long enough to do that, but his fingers dug into my thighs and pulled me up, positioning me the way he wanted. He teased me only for a moment, slowly licking my clit before he started to suck, holding me perfectly in the center of his mouth so that I didn't stand a chance. I shattered, and shattered . . . and shattered, as he alternated between sucking my clit and laving his tongue over me. He turned us over in a whoosh so that my back was pressed against the bed and he was on top of me, caging me as if I'd think to go anywhere. He brought his pelvis down, his cock rubbing against me as I whimpered, shook, completely wrung out but still spiraling with a need so great that my entire nervous system seemed to tremble with it.

"I need you to—"

"I know what you need," he said gravelly. I opened my eyes and met his, my heart pitter-pattering. How many times had I envisioned this moment? So many that it felt as if I'd summoned it to life, with him looking at me through hazy eyes, clouded with lust and something else, something that both terrified and excited me because I'd never seen him look at anyone else that way. He braced himself on either side of me and shifted so that his tip touched my folds. He thrust, and I gasped, arching, bracing myself, but he didn't push in. I frowned, looking up at him, realizing that I was completely panting.

"You need to calm down, sweetheart," he said in the sweetest voice, and I felt myself melt a little. Some of the pressure lifted from my shoulders as I breathed out and gave a little nod.

"Okay. I'm ready."

He watched me for a moment, his eyes searching mine. "You said you've done this before."

"Of course I have." I scoffed. "I'm twenty-four."

His eyes narrowed slightly, he moved again, pulling out completely and rubbing his pulsing cock over my clit. I bit my lip to keep from crying out, but holy moly my body was on fire.

"Tessa," he said. "Did you fuck that guy in college?"

"I did." I really did. I wasn't lying about that. It just may have been the one and only time I fucked anyone in college, though. His eyes searched mine rapidly.

He let out a slow breath that was followed by a string of curses as he rested his forehead on mine. "Was he the only time?"

"I've fooled around plenty of times," I said, offended. Just because I didn't have his experience didn't mean I didn't know what I was doing. I watched plenty of porn.

"I'm not saying it's a bad thing, baby," he whispered. "I just want to know how slow to take it."

"Just please, please, please, please, please fuck me."

That seemed to break through his uncertainty. He pushed himself inside me ever-so-slowly, torturously slowly, stretching me.

"You okay?"

I nodded, eyes wide, afraid to speak. He leaned down a bit and kept going, pushing deep and hard once until he was completely inside me.

"Fucking heaven, Tessa," he muttered against my neck. "You feel like fucking heaven."

I arched my back, wrapped my legs around his waist, and pushed against him. He cursed again. "If you keep doing that, I won't last. Swear to God, I won't." His words were choppy pants as he continued to thrust into me, slowly at first, so slowly I felt the burn spread through my veins and simmer as my eyes rolled back. Then, he picked up the movement and began to move faster, harder, his hand closing around my throat as he ground into me. For a moment, I feared I'd pass out from it—the hand, the way he was fucking me as if he never wanted to come up for air, the way his eyes stayed steady on mine as if he didn't care whether he did or not.

"Do you know how many time I pictured this?" he asked. "How many times I envisioned tearing off your clothes and fucking you like this?"

I moaned, feeling a spike of adrenaline shoot through my veins. My eyes rolled back. "Please don't stop."

"Never stopping." His fingers found my clit as he continued his thrusts. He was playing my body, and I sank into the rhythm of his hips, the strum of his fingers, the cadence of his words, and when I felt the build of my orgasm, the one I thought I wouldn't reach again after the one he gave me with his mouth, I reached for him, but he grabbed my wrists in one hand and held them over my head. My gaze dropped to the way the muscles in his abdomen contracted with each movement. When I looked back up, I focused on the clench of his jaw and the dark haze of lust in his eyes. He anchored me with that gaze, with his hand over my wrists, with every single motion of his ruthless fucking. He moaned, murmured something I couldn't quite capture as he moved a hand underneath my ass and, without pulling out, shifted so that he was sitting and I was straddling him. It was supposed to be a position that shifted the balance, the power, except Rowan still held it all. He held me as he fucked me from beneath. He held my gaze as he moved me up and down on his slippery, thick cock. He went in deeper this way, deeper in a way that stole my breath, my words . . . my thoughts.

"Tessa," he said over and over and over like a mantra. "My Tessa."

I'd never forget that. Not the way he said my name and not the way he looked at me as he said it. My heart felt like it was on the brink of exploding, and that was when I shattered around him, with his name spilling from my lips. He groaned mine out as he spilled himself inside me, pushing in with one final, hard motion, as to ensure I would never stop feeling him there. As our breaths recovered, he loosened his hold on me, and I untangled my legs from his waist. He blinked, looking at me with clear eyes, and brought his lips down to mine and kissed me again, softly, taking his time, saying things neither one of us would ever say aloud. And then we slept.

CHAPTER TWENTY-FIVE

WHY COULDN'T we have done this before? That was the first thought in my mind when I awoke with Rowan's fingers between my legs, stroking up and down my folds, flicking and circling over my sensitive clit. I moaned, blinking up at him. He was still looking at me with the same wondrous look as last night, the one that made my heart gallop. He slid first one and then two fingers into the well of my body, his eyes on mine as he worked them in and out. Expertly, he pulled sensations out of me until, silently, I climaxed because I couldn't seem to find my voice when he looked at me like that. He put his forehead on mine and breathed out before rolling over and getting out of bed. It was then that I realized he'd already showered and was halfway dressed. I cleared my throat.

"What time did you wake up?"

"I'm not sure I ever went to sleep." He pulled his shirt shut and worked on the buttons as he turned to face me.

"What do you mean?" I let my eyes drift over his body and sighed, making myself get out of bed.

He simply shrugged, turned away from me, and continued getting dressed. I headed to the bathroom. I showered and dressed quickly, taking a cue from him and wearing a black knee-length skirt, a button down, and heels. Comfortable heels. I threw a pair of flats in my bag just in case. I doubted Rowan intended to drive the car around the city, and if we were going to be on and off subways all day, I wouldn't want to be in heels. We ended up grabbing breakfast at a little deli on the corner. I tried not to focus on the way neither one of us seemed to know what to say, but it was impossible not to with the awkward silence climbing with each second that ticked by. Finally, deciding enough was enough, I put my cup of coffee on the table, lowered the newspaper he was covering his face with, and made him look at me.

"What is happening?"

"With what?" He eyed me, the newspaper, and me again.

"Well, I'm certainly not talking about the news."

He folded the paper carefully and set it aside. "I'm compart-mentalizing."

"Well, then." My brows rose. I hadn't exactly expected him to be that straightforward. "Compartmentalizing because you don't want to feel the emotion you're feeling?"

He nodded once in confirmation, and my heart skyrock-eted. A smile formed on my face, and I started to laugh even though none of this was funny. It was crazy and sad and definitely not humorous. His lips twitched as he watched me laugh at his expense. I just couldn't understand it. Maybe I didn't believe in love the way my sister did, not anymore anyway, after my parent's divorce, but I believed in something, and that something was close enough to love. It was what I'd always felt for Rowan, and for him to also possibly feel it but want to compartmentalize it instead of admit it was just . . . ugh. Frustrating. Once I gathered my wits, I took a breath and tried again.

"What do you normally do after you have sex with a woman?"

"Depends," he said. "I dated a couple of girls in college, but nothing serious, nothing that lasted very long. You know how I am." Shrug. "There was this one girl, she was on the track team. We went out a few times, had sex, and it kind of fizzled out."

"After a few times?" I knew my mouth was hanging open, but I couldn't help it. There was no way in hell I'd get tired of him in *just a few times*. "Did you get bored or did she?"

"I think we both did."

Impossible.

"What about you? Who was the guy?" he asked.

"Just some guy. We were at a party, and one thing led to another and we did it." I shrugged. Rowan's lips twisted as he looked at me as if he were trying to read more into my thoughts. I laughed a little. "I'm serious. There's really nothing much to tell. We had sex, I left, he went his own way, and that was that."

"Were you drunk?"

I pulled a face. "No."

"Was he?"

"No."

"Hm."

I took a deep breath and exhaled. "What?"

"What, what?" He shrugged nonchalantly, and I glared.

"Don't nonchalantly shrug at me," I said. "You're judging me."

"I am not judging you. Trust me. I'm not. I just wouldn't think you'd go and fuck the first guy who offered."

I scoffed, rolling my eyes. "You are judging, and he wasn't the first guy who offered. He was in my English class and I liked him. Seeing him at the party was just different. It was one of those moments you have when you're a kid and you see a teacher outside of school like they aren't allowed to have regular lives or something."

"Like the time we saw Mrs. Beers at the movies, and you asked her what she was doing there." His lip turned up at the mention of this. I smiled, feeling myself blush at the memory of my idiotic sixteen-year-old self (yes, sixteen, not four).

"Exactly."

"So, you saw each other at the party, had sex there, and went your separate ways?"

"Why do you look like you're tasting spoilt milk or something?"

"That's exactly how that thought of you with another man tastes in my mouth."

I shook my head, trying to play it off, but my heart was thumping erratically. He was jealous. Why did I like that so much? It was stupid of me, I knew it was.

"You never answered my question yesterday," he said.

"Which one?"

"Where do you see yourself in five years?"

"I don't know." I leaned back in my chair and looked out the window, watching the people swarm the streets as they tried to get to work.

"This may be your home soon," he said.

"Maybe."

"You deserve Paris."

I let out a laugh. "So I've heard."

"It's the fashion capital of the world."

"New York isn't that far behind it." I raised an eyebrow.

"But Paris, Tessa?" He got a twinkle in his eyes as they widened, like he was dreaming it for himself. "When will you get that opportunity again?"

He was right. I was just so tired of hearing it. I'd heard it from Freddie, Celia, Dad, Mom, Grandma Joan, and Sam.

"Are you done compartmentalizing? Can we get on our way and visit the factory now?"

He smiled, eyes dancing as he looked at me, and stood without another word. When we were walking outside, side by side, he wrapped an arm around me and said, "Thank you for last night and this morning."

I looked up at him, confused. "I didn't do anything this morning."

"You did."

"And last night? That was . . . both of us." I struggled to find words. I was still confused.

"You had only been with one guy," he explained. "And last night felt like . . . it felt like, you know."

"Like I was still a virgin?" I whispered. He nodded, eyes wide. It was so, so odd seeing him like this. So out of character. He was Rowan, captain of the rowing team, big muscular badass that women drooled over, always walking around like he had a place in the world, but these last two days had reverted him to his awkward stage when we were teenagers. It was just weird. I didn't know what to do with it.

"What is wrong with you?" I stopped walking, which made him stop walking. People bumped us from either side. Rowan took me by the arm and ushered me aside.

"What do you mean?"

"You're acting weird. Like, really weird. I don't know what to do with it."

He closed his eyes and let out a breath. When he opened them, he looked sure of himself again. Like a freaking programmed robot. But I didn't want the programmed robot. I wanted to know what the hell was happening in that brain of his. I grabbed his tie, looped it around my hand, yanked him closer to me, and kissed him hard. He groaned, his hand on my hair as he pushed me against whatever business was behind us. I heard someone holler for us to get a room and laughed into his mouth. He kissed me once more and backed away, his hungry gaze fixed on my slightly swollen lips.

"I forgot my pen in the hotel," he said.

"What?" I blinked. "Your pen?"

"It's a really special pen."

"Are you saying this so we can go have sex?"

"Really, really special pen," he murmured, his mouth coming down on mine again, his tongue doing the sweeping thing that hit me right between the legs. I nodded against him.

"Let's go back and get it."

CHAPTER TWENTY-SIX

ROWAN

OUR MINI-WORK VACATION WAS UP. We rode back home in mostly silence. It helped that Tessa was asleep half the time. It helped because it gave me time to think. To compartmentalize. To figuratively bash my head against the steering wheel as I drove while stealing glances of her sleeping form, the way I had done the last two nights. Like a creeper, basically. The deal was that I was freaking out. I never freaked out. Ever. I was calm, cool, collected. I did not bleed, for God's sake. I wasn't about to start. I took a breath and kept my eyes on the road. I didn't like feeling off-kilter. I'd felt it before, sure. Tessa seemed to be at the center of things every time I felt this way. It wasn't that I didn't like it, but I didn't know how to handle it. And honestly, as far as things went, this was horrific timing for me to try to even fathom bleeding. I shook the thought away. I really needed to stop thinking about blood like I was a fucking vampire or something.

"Where do you see yourself in five years?" Her voice startled me.

"I don't know."

"You don't know? You?" She scoffed. "I don't believe you."

"Where do you see me in five years?"

She tilted her head slightly, her lips pursing in a way that made me want to reach over and kiss her senseless. I looked back at the road ahead. Focus, Rowan. Focus.

"You'll be CEO of Hawthorne. You'll definitely have another location since you barely fit in the current one, maybe in New York? It's close enough, and it really is considered one of the fashion capitals of the world."

I shook my head, smiling. "Paris is still number one."

"Well, I don't think you're going to pick up and move to Paris."

"We have a headquarters in London."

"That's right," she said, as if the memory was coming back to her. "Your mom's. Is it still running?"

"It will be. Soon enough."

"Will you take over that as well?"

"I'll have to."

"Wow. Was that already in the works or is it also because of the divorce?"

"Yeah. They want to give me the company," I said. My heart clenched as if bracing for impact. "I guess the divorce isn't good for business."

"Not with the brand they've built." She rolled her eyes, smiling. She was right. My parents built this whole family-run company with the concept and selling point that family is the thread that holds people together. Cheesy and obviously unfit for us.

"They want me to get married."

She looked stricken. "To whom?"

"Anyone. I don't think they really care." Heat traveled down my spine. I scratched the back of my neck. "I mean, they care because there are a lot of specifics."

"Get married for what?"

"The family thing," I said. "You know."

"Wow." She blinked and then opened her eyes wide. "You're serious."

"Unfortunately."

"You don't even believe in love. How are you supposed to believe in marriage?"

"I don't have to believe in love or marriage. I just have to do it." I felt my jaw twitch and rubbed it, hoping the action would take away some of the ache I was feeling, but the ache was everywhere, in my jaw, the center of my chest, burning me from the inside out. I wasn't sure there was any solution to that, and seeing the way Tessa was reacting to this news wasn't making it any better.

"How?" She blinked a few times, as if trying to see me better. "I just . . . how?"

"It's a contract. I'd sign it like every other contract I sign, with the knowledge that I can always get out of it."

She folded her arms in front of her and looked out the window. We were two blocks away from her house, so I didn't push it. I didn't know what I would say to her anyway.

CHAPTER TWENTY-SEVEN

SHE DIDN'T ALLOW me to carry her bag for her, but I followed her to the door nonetheless. I didn't want this to end just yet. I wished I could find the words to say that, but she was visibly upset at me and I wasn't sure I could handle her throwing more things in my face right now.

"Thank you for coming with me."

She nodded as she unlocked the door. Nodded. Yeah, there was no chance I'd just leave right now. She walked inside, let go of the duffel bag and stood in the doorway, guarding it like Alfred in Batman, not quite trusting to let anyone in. It bothered me that the *anyone* was me. We had a perfectly enjoyable trip in every way imaginable. I knew the marriage thing probably came as a shock to her, but I didn't think she'd be angry about it. I felt myself frown.

"You're mad at me."

"I'm not." She lifted her face as she looked away briefly. "I'm disappointed. Though, I'm not sure why."

"Because you don't want me to get married." It was an obvious statement. I hadn't expected her face to crumble with it. Instantly, I wished I could take it back.

"I don't want you to get married for *those* reasons."

"It's just a contract."

"So you say."

"I'm not built for relationships, Tess. You know that better than anyone."

Her eyes narrowed. "Because you're afraid. If you do this, you really are going to end up like your parents. You're going to end up in a loveless marriage, and then you'll have to have kids with someone you don't love and . . ." She shook her head and exhaled, seemingly to catch her breath. I couldn't think of what to say, so I stayed quiet.

"Just say it. You're afraid." She was pushing, reaching. I sighed, running a hand through my hair.

"I'm not afraid of anything."

She shook her head, clear disappointment in her eyes. "Then there's nothing to talk about. I'll see you tomorrow morning in the office."

"Okay."

"Okay."

I hesitated. Then, she shut the door in my face.

I COULDN'T BREATHE. I woke in the middle of the night, clutching my chest, willing my breath to settle into my lungs. I'd joked with Tessa the other night, saying that she may kill me, but I hadn't intended on it actually happening. Telling her about the contract definitely did not go as planned. What was worse was that the entire time I was telling her about it, I had the question on the tip of my tongue. Maybe asking her would solve the issue. It would mean that at least I'd be stuck with somebody of my choosing. I'd have the most beautiful woman on my arm at every gala and every function we'd be required to attend on behalf of the company.

We'd take trips together and turn them into mini-honey-moons. I could picture my life with her. I'd told her it was just a contract, and it would be, but it would be a contract with some-body I actually enjoyed spending time with. I batted the thoughts aside. It was useless. Having her sign a contract would mean trap-ping her and ignoring the one thing she said she didn't want. She didn't want to be stuck here. She wanted to leave and be free. She wanted to chase her dreams in fashion design, and while I could try to make things work in a way in which she could still do that, it wouldn't be enough. She wouldn't have the dream apprentice-ship and eventually, little by little, she would start giving up tiny dreams until there were none left.

Reality settled in slowly, uncomfortably wedging its way under my breastbone, making its space right beside the possibility of what could be if things weren't already set in stone. If life wasn't dead-set on making it impossible for her and me to be together. I went back to bed and tossed and turned for another half hour before waking again and making my way to the bath-room, my chest squeezing tighter than before and breath barely escaping my lungs. I held on to the edge of the counter and focused on my intake of breath, deep and steady. If this was how I felt because I wasn't sleeping beside her, I didn't want to think about how great the loss would be when she walked away this time. I glanced up and looked at my reflection in the mirror.

Pale.

Drawn.

Desperate.

I needed to get ahold of myself, get a grip and go back to sleep. Maybe she'd pick the apprenticeship in New York. Maybe she'd stay close to home, close to me, and this wouldn't have to end.

My mind went back to my previous thoughts, the ones I thought I'd talked myself out of already. Maybe . . . maybe I could figure out a different way to bring up the stupid marriage certificate I needed and the pretend wife that would need to be by my side during some of the company launches. No one would understand it better than she would. Tessa knew me on another level, one that no one else had reached. Surely, I could make her understand why I needed to do this.

And then what? She'd agree to be your wife and play house with you, all the while knowing you'd never tell her you love her, never let her feel how much you need her?

I pounded my fist on the sink and cursed. She deserved better than that. She deserved Paris.

With that thought, I washed my face and went back to bed a third time.

CHAPTER TWENTY-EIGHT

TESSA

I DIDN'T KNOW why this bothered me. I didn't believe in marriage at all, but for some reason, talking about it like it was a contract and not a sacrament made me feel a little sick. And his whole stance on relationships? It was bullshit. He was perfectly fine in relationships as long as he tricked himself into believing he wasn't in one. He was loving and kind and attentive and all the things anybody could ever want in a boyfriend. He just wasn't willing to be a boyfriend. If I pointed that out, it would only make the argument worse and more complicated, which would only rile me up more than I already was, so I went another route.

I called my sister. Why I called her will forever be a mystery to me. Probably because, despite being the worst person ever to take relationship advice from, she was still my sister and best friend. And because midnight my time meant it was morning her time. It wasn't odd for me to be awake in the middle of the night either, so Celia answered the phone as if I did this every day.

"What's up?"

"Nothing."

"Hm." She paused. I could hear the frown in her voice. "Spill it. What's happening? Is it Rowan?"

"What? Why would you assume that?"

"Because every time you sound like this, it's because he's done something." Another pause. "Wait. Is it the apprenticeship? Have you decided? Did you tour NYC?"

She said it like that. N-Y-C. I sighed. "It's Rowan."

"Knew it. What'd he do or not do now?"

"Well, for starters, he did me." I covered my face with my free hand. "That sounds so weird."

"Oh shit," she gasped. "Hold on one second. I'm going to step outside so I can hear you better." I heard her heels clicking against the floor, a door open and close, and her breath huffed into the line. "Talk to me."

"Well, we went to New York on a business trip, right, and it went really well. We talked about hooking up while I was home—"

"Wait a minute. You discussed hooking up?"

"Yeah." I squeezed my eyes shut. "I know."

"Only Rowan, dude."

"I know. I think he was just afraid that we'd hook up and go our separate ways again and I'd hate him because of it. Who knows?" I shrugged at my own thoughts.

"He's so . . . particular. Did he also discuss what kind of condoms he uses with you or was that left off the check list?"

I bit my lip. I didn't need a mirror to tell you my face was the color of a tomato.

"Oh my god, Tessa, tell me you used a condom."

"I'm on the pill." I rolled my eyes.

"You are the worst pill taker in the history of pill taking," she said. "You can't even remember to take your vitamins!"

"I'm fine. Chill out."

"I hope you know what you're doing," she said and proceeded to pray to some saint.

"You aren't even Catholic."

"In times like these, I pull from all religions."

I scoffed. "Stop it."

"Okay. I'm done being dramatic. What happened after you had sex?"

I launched into everything, starting at the cocktail party and ending with him telling me he needed to get married if he wanted to take over the company. When I finished, I was met with silence. "Celia?"

"Yeah, I'm here, I just . . . that's a lot to take in."

"I know."

"You can't do this for him, Tess," she whispered after a while. "I know you've always had a thing for him and you want to save the world and everyone in it, but that isn't your job. You need to live your life too."

"He didn't ask me to help him. He didn't even hint at me playing the role of fake wife."

"But it bothers you to think about someone else doing it?"

I shrugged in the dark. Obviously, it bothered me. I was calling her about it in the middle of the night. "I guess."

"Don't do anything stupid. If you get stuck there, you'll

resent yourself and you'll end up resenting him. I think Rowan knows that."

"I don't know that I would resent him."

"You would. Look at Mom. Look at Grandma Joan. Look at every single woman you've ever met who was forced to give up a part of herself at one point in her life for a man."

"So, basically all women," I said. "We all give up something."

She paused. "Yeah, I guess you're right. Still, you're too young to do that right now. He isn't your responsibility, and you know he'd make an awful husband. He doesn't know the first thing about love."

I wanted to argue with her. I wanted to tell her she was wrong and that the statement wasn't true. Rowan was kind-hearted and thoughtful. He could make a great husband if he wanted to. But that was where the problem lay. He didn't want to, and I wasn't sure that would ever change. The doorbell rang before I got the chance to say anything at all. I sat up quickly.

"Was that the doorbell?"

"Yeah." I got out of bed, slid my feet into my fuzzy sandals, and made my way downstairs. "Don't hang up," I whispered to my sister.

"Obviously not. Who the hell is there at this time? Isn't it almost one in the morning there?"

"Yeah." I pressed to my tiptoes, looked through the peephole, and frowned. "It's Rowan."

"What the hell?"

I stayed on my toes and inspected him better. He was wearing a black T-shirt that stretched over his expansive chest, his hair was in disarray, and his expression was completely blank. I heard my sister's protest as I hung up the phone and pulled the door open slowly.

"What are you—"

He stepped forward, cupped the back of my neck, and crashed his mouth to mine.

CHAPTER TWENTY-NINE

ROWAN

I WAS BEING IMPULSIVE. When had I ever been this impulsive? I broke apart from her lips when I felt her hands on my chest, pushing me away. Her eyes opened slowly, as if in a daze, which was exactly how I felt.

"What are you doing here?"

I pressed my forehead to hers, closed my eyes, and breathed against her in a plea, begging her not to let go, not yet. I wished I could summon the words to my lips, but it would be no use. Even if I could speak the words aloud, I wouldn't. I shouldn't.

It isn't fair to her, Rowan.

None of this was. Yet, there I stood, wishing for things that wouldn't come true.

"Just give me two days, Tess," I managed to say against her lips. "Two days, no holds barred. Just us."

She pulled back slightly, her eyes searching mine. I could tell she wanted to say yes. I wanted to pull the words out of her. Instead, I held my breath and awaited her response.

"Two days?" she asked, holding my gaze steady. I nodded. "That seems so little for something so big."

I fought a grin, fought the stupid, childish comment of, "That's what she said."

She'd laugh, I knew she would, but this wasn't the time for jokes.

"You're leaving in three, aren't you?"

"Yeah. That's the plan." She exhaled.

"So give me two days."

"No holds barred means you'll have to tell me your deepest, darkest secrets."

"As long as you tell me yours."

She licked her lips and smiled. "Deal."

"Deal."

And then my lips were on hers again.

CHAPTER THIRTY

TESSA

WE WERE LYING on my mattress in my nearly empty room. Even with all of my childhood furniture gone, I was trying hard not to be weirded out, especially not after he'd just had his mouth, his hands, his body all over and inside mine. He propped himself on his elbow and faced me. I was still breathing heavily from the orgasm he'd just given me, but my eyes were open, looking at the popcorn ceiling.

"Why do they texture ceilings?" I said. "It's so pointless."

"Is that really what you want to talk about right now?"

No, it wasn't, but I also didn't want to look at him just yet.

"No holds barred," he reminded me and tapped my temple three times. Tap, tap, tap. "What's going on up there?"

"I just can't believe you'd get married," I whispered. I felt him stiffen beside me and knew he was probably wishing he hadn't gotten off the ceiling topic, but I couldn't leave it alone. The idea had haunted me since he'd told me about it. "What if you happen to meet the woman of your dreams, and you're wasting time by being married to another one just for the sake of a contract?"

He laid his head beside mine. His breath tickled my nipple when he spoke again. "Do you really think it's likely that I'd meet someone like that?"

"You never know."

"That wouldn't happen." He shook his head. "I know it wouldn't."

"But how do you know?" I pushed back, needing space to think and desperately wanting to look into his eyes. The second I did, I regretted it. His sad and hollow expression hit me deep in my marrow, and not for the first time, I wasn't sure I could be the one to fix this brokenhearted man.

"People like me aren't meant to fall in love. We aren't meant for others to fall in love with us either. I'm too closed off, too guarded, too . . . I just . . . you know how people talk about the perfect match?" He shifted onto his elbow. I mimicked the movement. "I don't want that to ever be true for me because my perfect match would be hollow and afraid, and I don't want to ever have to see that version of myself."

I wasn't sure what to do with his confession, so I said nothing. I'd always thought your perfect match was supposed to complement you in every way, but what did I know about perfect matches? The only thing I knew for certain was that the mere thought of him being like this with somebody else felt like a stab to my chest. His gaze broke away from mine and landed on my exposed breasts. I resisted the urge to pull the blanket back up.

"I feel shy," I whispered, closing my eyes away from his heated gaze.

"Shy?" He chuckled, that deep sound that did crazy things to me. His nose flicked mine, and he said, "Open your eyes," against my lips with this soft, gravelly voice that made my heart pitter-patter a little too hard for my comfort, so I took my time complying.

"I think we need the lights off."

"I disagree." He moved so that I could see all of him, but it also meant he could see all of me, which he had already done in New York. Why was this so embarrassing? I felt a flush creep up on my face. "I want to look at you."

"You don't need to look at me to fuck me."

"But I want to."

"I hate you right now." I groaned, fighting the urge to shut my eyes.

He grinned, eyes dancing. "Liar."

"I'm not lying, and I seriously hate you right now."

"Hm. Come here, baby." He leaned in and bit my bottom lip, sucked it into his mouth. He grabbed me with ease and positioned me so I was straddling him, his hard length between us as he took in every inch of me. "Show me how much."

My heart pounded as I braced myself on his chest and sank down on him. This time, I did close my eyes, savoring the feeling and trying to control the moan that threatened to come out as he stretched me, filled me so completely. I found my rhythm, slow at first. Gliding over him, I threw my head back every time his thrust met mine and his pubic bone tapped my clit. Then he grabbed my ass and spread me, his hips coming up harder, faster, making me feel wilder, out of control. I lifted my knees and picked up the pace, bracing myself on his strong, thick thighs as his hands slid up my body, as his palms cupped my breasts, as his fingers rolled my nipples.

"Oh God," I moaned.

"Yes," he hissed right before he flipped me without so much as losing his rhythm. I was panting for breath, my legs over his shoulder and he entered me again, slowly, so slowly I thought I'd vanish before he completely stretched me. I whimpered when he stopped moving, let out a harsh breath, and looked down at me, his hair swirling onto his forehead, bobbing with his blinks.

"Okay?"

I nodded, lips parted as I looked up at him, my heart pounding so hard I was sure it would end up inside his chest instead of mine. When he brought his face down and slanted his mouth on mine in a slow, tender kiss, my heart stopped beating all together. He bit my lower lip as he thrust deeper into me. My breath hitched, my back arched with the torturous movement. He seemed to be pacing himself, or maybe just enjoying tormenting me by not giving me what I wanted. I wrapped my legs around his waist and lifted myself, pressing into him. His gaze found mine in a gasp, and for a moment, neither one of us moved. Then he started to fuck me, spreading my legs farther apart, gripping my inner thighs harder with each thrust. My back arched into his movements. I wasn't sure how much more of it I could take. I wasn't sure how much . . . his hand came down between us and found my clit, stroking it as he fucked me. His free hand moved to cup my breast, his fingers pinching and rolling my nipple. Sensation seared through my veins as we found our pace. I felt like a furnace from the inside, hot with each lick of the wildfire that seemed to consume me. He whispered my name, a vow, a pledge. I moaned out his with pleasure as I went over the edge and looked into his eyes as he bit his lip and spiraled down with me.

CHAPTER THIRTY-ONE

THE FOLLOWING MORNING, I wasn't surprised to find that he wasn't there. My first thought was: he got scared.

Hell, I was scared.

What we'd shared was nothing short of magical in my book. Still, I would've liked for him to have stayed. I reminded myself that it was a workday. I was sure he'd gone home, showered, changed. I did the same, wondering if he still wanted me to go into the office. I figured I would. I could continue making calls and setting up appointments and phone calls for him today and tomorrow. It was two more days on the paycheck. I told myself it was only that. I'd agreed to two weeks, and I wouldn't cut it short. I turned around, keys in one hand and phone in the other as I scrolled for an Uber when I heard a car pull up, the gravel of my driveway crunching beneath its tires. Goosebumps kissed their way up my arms as I locked the door. I didn't have to turn around to know it was him. I pushed the side button on my phone, Uber ignored, and watched as he pulled to a stop in front of me, passenger window down.

"You're going to be late," he called out.

"You think my boss will be upset?" I opened the door and slid into the seat, snapping on my seatbelt before facing him. His gaze was dark and needy as he leaned in, put a hand behind my neck, and pulled me closer.

"Furious," he responded against my lips.

My heart bounced in anticipation of his kiss, which I didn't have to wait long for. His tongue swept into my mouth and play alongside mine in a deep, slow tango that made me think about hard, slow, fucking. I clenched my thighs in response, moaned against his mouth, caught a fistful of his hair as I pulled him even closer. We were both breathing heavily when we broke the kiss, him nibbling on my lower lip, me tugging his into my mouth and extracting a rumbled sound from him that made my pulse kick.

"Your dad's going to be mad at you," I whispered when he placed his forehead against mine. I felt him smile against my lips. He kissed me one more time and settled back into his driving position.

"I brought an overnight. I didn't really want to leave you this morning, but I didn't want to wake you up either." He handed me a coffee and a bag from the coffee shop down the street. I peeked in and pulled out the bagel.

"You stayed over?" I didn't know why this surprised me. "I didn't really peg you for the staying over type."

"I stayed over the other night."

"We didn't have sex that night."

"Which makes staying over weirder if you think about it."

"I guess."

"And we shared a hotel room in New York."

"Exactly. Shared hotel rooms imply that we're both staying over." I looked out the window as I added, "Preferably having sex."

"Preferably, huh?" I could hear the smile in his voice, but I didn't face him since I was trying to hide my own. "I came over last night because I wanted to sleep with you."

I turned my attention to him. "Obviously."

"Just sleep with you," he clarified. "The sex . . . the sex was incredible, don't get me wrong, but I hadn't planned on that."

"You pounced me the minute I opened the door."

His smile was almost bashful. *Almost.* "I couldn't help myself."

"Hm."

By the time we pulled up to the Hawthorne building, we were both grinning. Rowan went to the office to get ready for his morning meeting with his dad while I went over to Sam's cubicle. He took in my appearance with a smile when he saw me approach.

"How was the trip?"

"It was . . . good."

"You seem happier today."

"Do I?" I leaned against the partition wall, still grinning. "Why don't you have an office?"

"Like Mighty Rowan with the office and the girl?"

I rolled my eyes. "You never wanted the girl."

He paused for a moment too long for comfort, his eyes scanning my face that way he did when he wanted to say something but was afraid of the consequences. I held my breath. No, no, no damn it. We went over this. We'd kissed and decided there was nothing there. But then, does a simple kiss determine your feelings for a person you've known your entire life?

"Sam," I started. He shook his head, tearing his gaze from mine.

"Ignore me. I'm being a brat." He sat on the edge of his desk, and I willed my feet to walk over to him, to be there for him.

"What's going on?"

He sighed heavily. "I haven't been feeling well lately, and it's making me act like a pansy."

"You aren't a pansy." I smiled, opened my mouth to make a joke, but then stopped myself and took a seat next to him on his desk. "What do you feel? Have you been to the doctor?"

"Just tired. All the time. My vision is fucked up. My head hurts. I think I need glasses."

"Glasses, Sam?" I laughed. "Dude. Go get glasses! You stare at a computer all day."

"I'm going this week." He shot me a weak smile. "Have you decided? Paris or New York?"

"I'll go to New York on Monday and tour the place and then do the same for Paris on Wednesday before I decide."

"You realize how rare that is, right?"

I nodded and swallowed the emotion threatening to bubble up. I knew it was rare. My friend Hannah was still trying to get an apprenticeship somewhere, and she was talented as hell. I knew I was talented, and I'd been sending designs to both companies since I was in high school, so it wasn't completely outlandish that I'd applied to both when it came time, thinking I'd maybe, possibly, only get one. I was as shocked as anyone when I received phone calls from both offering me the position of my dreams.

I pushed off the desk and gave Sam a side hug. He put his arm around me and rested his head on top of mine.

"You'll tell me when you decide, right? You won't disappear again."

"I won't disappear again."

"Good."

Just then, we heard the elevator open and straightened as Camryn appeared. My heart pounded hard in my chest. She was dressed in one of those form-fitting shift dresses that not many people could pull off. It hung perfectly on her super slim body, those gazelle legs of hers carrying her weightlessly across the room. She glanced over to where we were and waved with a warm smile and finally approached. With Camryn, I never knew what version I was getting—the candied bubblegum girl or the vicious viper that lay beneath. I braced myself for both. She shot her megawatt smile at Samson first.

"I missed you at family dinner last night."

Family dinner? Did the Hawthornes really hold up pretenses even when there were no longer any to hold up? It wouldn't surprise me if they did.

"Didn't feel like I needed to be there," he said. "Not much of a family."

Her brows pulled in slightly. "That isn't fair, Sam. Just because your parents aren't happy with each other doesn't mean they don't love their children."

"My father has multiple children," he said. "He has us and one with another woman."

I felt the breath go out of me, and I could tell Camryn was just as shocked as I was. We shared a look, probably one of the only looks of solidarity we'd ever shared.

"Rowan hasn't mentioned . . ."

"Yeah, why would he?" Sam said. "I'm just saying, it isn't insane that neither one of us show up for their stupid, pretentious family dinner." He held his temple as he said the words. I reached into my bag and fished out some ibuprofen. I rattled the little container, which he took from me.

"What are you doing here anyway?" he asked Camryn after he finished swallowing his pills.

"I have a meeting with your dad and Rowan."

"A meeting." Sam's words hung between the three of us like thick fog.

"Yep." She smiled suddenly and looked at me, tilting her head slightly. "I heard you're still drawing dresses."

"Here and there." I pushed the words out quickly, hoping that would be the last of her questions. She stared at me for a long time, her clear blue eyes glittering. Her go-to look when she wanted someone to cower before her. I held my ground. Truth was, I hadn't sketched much lately. For some odd reason, inspiration only hit me when I felt alone. Who would have ever guessed that? Inspiration for wedding dresses hitting someone when they were alone and single felt like the worst kind of irony.

"I'd love to see them," she said finally. "The wedding dresses, I mean. I may be in the market for one."

It wasn't her words but the slow smile that bloomed on her face that did me in. Rowan's words rushed into my memory. His parents wanted him to get married for the sake of the company. Someone had to be the sacrificial lamb. I tried hard to cling on to the last shred of self-control I had left. She was baiting me. I shouldn't take the bait.

Don't bite. Don't bite. Don't bite.

I summed a smile.

"Someone like you would never walk down the aisle wearing any less than Vera Wang," I said before turning to Sam. "I promised Rowan I'd get some work done before I left. Hope you feel better." I looked at Camryn as I sidestepped her. "Good luck with the dress."

Heart pounding, emotions rattling, I walked away.

"We're going in the same direction," she said behind me. I heard her heels click on the tile as she caught up to me. "Have you managed to sell the house? I saw a sign up yesterday."

"Not yet. Hopefully soon." We rounded the corner and neared Rowan's office. I pushed the door open. He was standing, hunched over some papers, and didn't look up right away.

"Hey, have you seen my—" His brows pinched. "What are you doing here?"

Camryn sidestepped me and went around the desk. He stood at his full height, a good half foot taller than she was, and she was damn tall with those graceful, thin legs. If I didn't hate her so much, I'd kill to dress her. I watched as she threw her arms around his neck. He grabbed her by the shoulders and put distance between them, shooting me a quick look to make sure I knew he wanted no part of it. The damage was done. I walked to my desk and sat with my back facing them as I clicked the mouse and powered my computer to life.

"Ro," she said, sweet valley girl voice. "Today's our meeting with Alistair, remember? Father said I needed to come right away to talk about the . . . the contract."

The contract. I bit my lip. The fucking marriage that one of them held as nothing more than a contract and the other was happier than a pig in shit to oblige by. Maybe I'd talk to him. Maybe I'd try to talk him out of the stupidity he was about to commit to. And then what? Suggest I marry him instead? A shiver shot through me. It would still only be a contract to him and I would give up everything, for what? Because I was holding on to some schoolgirl notion that I could make him love me? No thank you.

"Let's get this over with," he grumbled. I continued clicking the document in the computer in front of me and picked up the phone, dialing Spain. They walked out wordlessly, and I pulled the curtain slightly to watch as they walked to Alistair's office across the hall. Camryn was looking up at him, making a joke that clearly wasn't amusing him at all. Then she reached and pinched his butt. He continued walking. That tiny gesture was the crutch of all of it. It wasn't that he'd ever shown extreme interest in her, it was that he did absolutely nothing to stop her advances.

CHAPTER THIRTY-TWO

TESSA

Past

I LOOKED into the cup of punch in my hand and wished it were spiked. Corrigan was standing beside me going on and on about the branches of the military. Freddie deployed about a month ago, and since then, it has been all everyone wanted to talk about. It was as if no one understood why a guy who had everything going for him—money, looks, women—would choose to go and fight for his country rather than take the comfortable route. It was as if they'd all forgotten nine-eleven and how torn up we all were when it happened. It hadn't even been two years, for God's sake. I'd be lying if I said I didn't worry sick over my brother's safety, but I was prouder of him than anyone else in my family. I glanced up and watched as my parents spoke to Mildred. Mom had her hand on her chest, her eyes caked with anti-inflammatory cream and makeup to try to hide her distress, and Dad was nodding along to whatever was being said.

My brother's deployment had added ten years to their state, and my Yale acceptance had added another ten. Funny how that worked. They'd pushed for me to go there, and I could have sworn that they wished they could take it all back, whether it was because I was the youngest and would be out of the house soon or because they realized how steep the tuition was, I wasn't sure. They never outright said anything other than they were happy for me. Nevertheless, uneasiness rested in the things we didn't say, and they weren't saying anything at all. Ever. Not to me and not to each other. The only time they seemed to interact was when we were in social settings like these.

"So, yeah, if I joined any, it would be the Coast Guard," Corrigan said. I shot him a look.

"You're still talking about this?"

"You tuned me out, didn't you?"

"Sorry. There's only so much armed forces talk I can handle, especially with my brother flying jets over enemy territory." I took a sip of my punch. "Maybe we should raid the alcohol cabinet."

"Let's go."

We walked inside and went downstairs to the basement where Alistair kept the good stuff. Not that we knew what good stuff was. We always went for the vodka, rum, or tequila without a second glance at the label.

"So you and Ro are over," Corrigan commented as he poured vodka into our punch glasses.

"Did we ever really begin?"

He looked up without fully turning his face toward me. "Don't undermine me."

"I'm not." I took the glass he handed me and clinked it against his in a toast. "I just wouldn't exactly call what we were doing a relationship or even a hook up. Maybe a casual messing around."

I was lying through my teeth, and I was sure Corrigan knew it. There was nothing casual about Ro and me, especially right before he ended things. We'd been inseparable, just not important enough for him not to break up with me because he was leaving. I tried to contain the pang in my chest when I thought about it. His breakup had been methodical, simple and clean, the way skilled surgeons cut through skin. I'd been expecting it, so I'd handled it okay. I smiled up at Cor as we went upstairs.

"You'd call finally taking your relationship with quite arguably your best friend a casual hook up?" Cor said. I blinked up at him.

"What would you call it?"

"Love."

"Love? Are you insane?" I spit some of my drink back into my cup because I didn't want to spray the furniture.

"Right. I forgot you two have sworn off love." He shook his head, eyes rolling. "You're both full of shit."

Maybe I was full of shit, but Rowan wasn't. He genuinely didn't believe in love and I didn't want to be the girl who fell in love with the guy unwilling to reciprocate it. So yeah, maybe I was full of shit, but I was also doing the best I could to guard my own heart from it all, and with good reason.

"Because we don't believe in love?"

"Because you don't believe you're in love."

"We aren't."

"He asked you to go to Columbia for him."

"Yet, I'm going to Yale."

"Why is that?" We walked back outside and joined the party again. It wasn't much of a party. There was no loud music or drunken people jumping in the pool, not like the real parties we'd had when there weren't any parents around. As Rowan liked to say, it was an adult, classy party. My heart hurt a little when I thought about all the things he liked to say, and it hurt a little more when I thought of all the things he refused to say.

"Yale has always been my dream. If he really wanted to be with me, if he really wanted to . . . whatever, he would have gone to my first-choice school."

"He got a scholarship."

"An athletic scholarship," I corrected. "He could've applied to Yale."

"He did."

"Oh. I wasn't aware." I deflated a little. Why had Rowan never told me that he'd applied?

"Bet you never asked."

I hadn't asked. I'd just assumed Rowan was trying to be Rowan and get his way by making me apply to his college of choice instead of him applying to mine. The realization made my heart sink a little. Would he have gone if he'd been accepted? Would I have switched knowing he'd at least tried? I shook the thoughts away. It was too late for the answers to matter.

"I'd never ask him to give up rowing for me. He shouldn't ask me to give up Yale for him."

We stood there in silence. Sam joined us shortly after.

"You spiked your drinks?" he asked, standing in front of us. Corrigan and I lifted our glasses and smiled. Sam shook his head. "Bastards."

"You're still set on the tech college?" Cor asked Sam.

"Dude, you ask me this every time you see me," Sam said. "And you literally see me every fucking day."

"Hey, someone needs to care," Corrigan said. "Bet your parents don't ask."

Sam chuckled. "Damn straight."

He went on to talk about his classes—again, not that I minded. He loved it, and it was as if something sparked to life inside him when he talked about the creative aspect of it all. I loved hearing it because I was going to Yale to study the same thing. The only difference was a mortgage-size loan. No biggie.

I broke away from the conversation to get myself an hors d'oeuvre and almost turned right back around when I spotted a dark blue dress from the corner of my eye. I hoped Mildred wasn't coming over to talk to me. It wasn't that I didn't like her. It was that we had virtually nothing in common. Mildred was rock hard in every possible way, cold, calculating and so unlike my mother, who was soft and emotional, maybe too emotional at times. To be honest, it was a wonder how Dad had put up with her for this long, but who was I to judge? I smelled Mildred's staple Chanel perfume as she approached, and I lowered the small spinach quiche from my mouth before I took a bite.

"You look lovely today," she commented.

"As do you." I smiled. "Are you ready to have the house to yourself again? No more rampant rowers messing up your furniture."

"I'm . . . conflicted about it," she said. My brows shot up. She never, ever said things like that, but then, Rowan was her favorite, and unlike most mothers, Mildred unabashedly played favorites. We both tore our gazes away from each other's at the same time, looking out to the party. I followed the loud laughter I heard, the one that made my heart skip a beat, and looked at Rowan, who was talking to Camryn.

"I wanted to thank you," Mildred said beside me. I looked at her again. She was watching Rowan. "For not going to Columbia."

"Oh?" My heart thundered. "I'm surprised you even know about that."

"Oh, you know, I've heard the guys talking here and there." She glanced at me, her eyes showing no sign of emotion. "You would have ruined his life. And your own."

"How so?"

"You aren't a good fit for Rowan, dear. You're plain and childish and, quite frankly, I don't understand what my son sees in you." Her tone was so thick with feigned regret I was surprised she didn't choke on it. "He belongs with that girl. Someone who will make him see the bigger picture. Who will explore the world with him and build the company up, not tear it down or settle for some cutesy little family."

I felt myself clam up at her words. This woman had welcomed me into her house with open arms. She'd smiled at me and asked how I was doing. She'd pretended to care about my family and me. How could she say those things? I willed the tears to stop building in my eyes. I couldn't give her the satisfaction of seeing she'd gotten to me. I tried to remind myself of what a royal bitch she was to her own sons, but it wasn't much help, the ache of her words was still there, sitting in my chest. Instead, I made myself look at Rowan and Camryn again. They'd never been a couple, but they'd always managed to look like one. Maybe it was their Greek god and goddess good looks, both tall and effortlessly classic. Something akin to jealousy wedged its way inside my chest. I found it increasingly difficult to breathe as I watched them, but I couldn't tear my gaze away. Just the other day, we'd kissed. Just the other day, he'd looked at me as if I were his world. Just the other day, his fingers were inside me, my mouth was on him until he climaxed. Just the other day, he broke things off, saying a long distance "whatever this was" would never work. I'd agreed. He was right, of course. I'd been understanding and kissed him feverishly and then walked away, wondering if he wanted me to fight. But I didn't want to fight or be fought for. Mildred walked away from me without another word. Whether it was because she saw that I couldn't summon my own response or because she got bored, I wasn't sure. I didn't care.

Sam and Cor joined me again.

"That was harsh," Corrigan said.

"I am so sorry," Sam added.

"Not your fault." I shrugged, not having realized they were listening and also not willing to show just how much I was dying inside. "Perhaps she's right, anyway."

Neither one of them agreed or disagreed. It was the thing I hated about having male friends. Women would stand by you, they'd be mad with you, sad with you, stomp the ground for you, and curse the world for you. Men just stood there helplessly. It annoyed me. I set my glass down, threw away the quiche I no longer wanted, and said goodbye to them. I was halfway to the sidewalk when I heard someone running behind me and turned around. My heart spiked at the sight of Rowan in his slacks, button-down shirt, and tie. He ran a hand through his hair and stopped in front of me.

"I leave at six in the morning."

"I know." I swallowed.

"You aren't gonna say goodbye?"

"We already said goodbye a few weeks ago, did we not?" I said. "Besides, you were busy with your girlfriend."

A flash of something claimed his features—regret, panic? Just like inside, I refused to let the hurt rise to my features.

"She isn't my girlfriend," he said. Stupid, idiotic excuse.

"He belongs with that girl."

Tears burned in my eyes. Hot, stupid, annoying tears. I blinked them away quickly.

"No one is," I whispered. "You don't bleed."

His eyes flashed when I said this. He'd thought I'd forgotten. He thought that because we were high when he told me that whole bit about his father and the way he made him continuously repeat that mantra that I could ever forget it. But how could I? It was terrifying and sad and everything wrong with the world, and it was something he'd been taught since he was a kid.

"I don't," he confirmed.

"I know."

He cupped my face, and for maybe the last time, he looked at me as if I were the world. Like I was the sun and he was locked in my orbit. He opened his mouth to say something and closed it again, came closer still, lowered his face to mine, and kissed me. It was a soft kiss filled with regret and goodbyes, and when I walked away from him that time, I felt my heart crack open a little. I told myself I didn't bleed either. But I was wrong.

CHAPTER THIRTY-THREE

ROWAN

Present

FOR AS LONG as I could remember, I'd hated my father, but I'd never hated him more than that very moment. I sat in his office with Camryn beside me and our lawyer beside her, listening to their points as to why she'd be perfect for the contractual wife role. They had good points, I'd give them that. The reason the meeting was taking longer than usual, was because I'd spent a full hour arguing the point. Camryn just stood there, stoic, letting me say awful things about her without a care in the world, showing me why she was truly cut out for this role. I fought it as much as I could.

I said that I would never in a million years marry a selfish, bratty, mean girl. Camryn laughed at the last bit, her green eyes sliding to mine with humor and absolutely no shame.

"You don't have to be in love with me. Have you not been paying attention? This isn't about love or selflessness."

That shut me up. I sat there and listened the rest of the time. We were both incapable of loving people the way they wanted to be loved, and we knew that. I listened as the lawyer lectured her about the possibility of signing the marriage contract and what it entailed. She nodded and listened intently, asking questions every so often. How much money would she get at the end of all of it? What if she wanted to end the marriage? Could we add a no-children clause in the contract? Questions that made it clear she really was perfect for this role. She didn't want involvement; she wanted money. She wanted to keep her independence, probably screw around with the Wall Street guy, and be able to travel while cashing her check for being married to me. I couldn't blame her for not wanting a real marriage. I didn't either.

"You have to be sure about this Camryn," Dad said in his warm tone that held a hint of warning. "The idea is for you to be married forever, but if divorce is something you're dead-set on from the start, I have to warn you that you won't be able to get out of this for at least a few years."

She put her hand on mine over my knee. What should have been a comforting gesture felt like claws sinking into my skin. I calmly took her hand, set it on the armrest, and leaned forward, taking a set of papers from my father's desk.

"I'm okay with that," she said with a casual shrug. "I mean, that's all marriage is anyway, right? A contract."

"For some people, it can be more than that."

My eyes rose to meet my father's. I glared. "Let's stick to the contracts."

"Very well."

The lawyer continued to explain everything, and each word felt like another cement block dragging me deeper into a bottomless lake. Sweat broke out across my brow, down my spine, and I reached up and wiped my forehead. It wasn't a good adrenaline, not like when I was about to start a rowing meet. This was . . . I wasn't sure what this was. It was something I definitely hadn't felt before. I was comfortable enough with Camryn. I'd known her since we were in diapers. Sure, when we were in public, she could sometimes be a little much with the displays of affection, but in private, she was just an insecure girl trying to navigate her way through life.

"If it's okay, I'd like to have my lawyer look at these before I sign," she said.

We all agreed. The lawyer put copies in a folder and gave them to her, explaining that it was also imperative she understood the clauses in the pre-nuptial and noted things she wanted added before we proceeded. She said her goodbyes, stood, and left. The lawyer followed. Then it was only my father and I sitting in a cold office.

"You're sure about this," Dad said.

"You haven't given me much of a choice."

"You have a choice in whom you marry," he said. "It doesn't have to be all business."

"And that was why you brought Camryn in? Because I have a choice?" I asked dryly.

He sighed heavily. "That isn't fair, Rowan. You want to be the head of the company. You want to make the big decisions and drive it forward. This is what needs to be done. Camryn is a good candidate because she knows what's expected, and look, she wants a three- to four-year contract, which furthermore shows you that she's only in this for the business aspect of it. Once it's done, you can have a shot at something real. I hope you find that someday."

I shook my head, looking away from him. I'd grown up with two emotionless parents who didn't give a shit about my and my brother's feelings.

"You never gave a shit before," I said. "We don't bleed, remember?"

"I'm trying here, Rowan." He exhaled heavily, shutting his eyes. "I've made a lot of mistakes. Mariah—"

I stood, done with this conversation, and reached the door before turning around and looking at him.

"Maybe you should teach your other kid the mistakes you've made. It's rather late to repair the damage you caused to Sam and me."

With that, I walked back to my office. I opened the door and took a nice, deep breath at the sight of Tessa. She glanced up quickly and went right back to her phone call and computer screen, but not before I saw the flash of agony in her expression. I sat behind my desk and alternated between staring at the back of her head and closing my eyes to listen to the sound of her voice, which was light and bubbly when she spoke to the account managers in Europe. The genuine laughter she shared with them had the crushing weight on my chest lifting a bit.

Eventually, I managed to type out an email, and as soon as I hit send, my eyes found the back of her head again, the long, soft, brown curls I'd been running my fingers through last night. I wanted to get up and run my fingers through them again, feel the lightness. I wanted to drag my lips down her neck and body. I wanted to make her feel this unsettling feeling I was harboring for her, for my situation.

My father could even go as far as making the claim that he didn't want me to end up like him, but it was too late. I was exactly like him. I was selfish and driven by success and would marry a woman like Camryn—one that wouldn't hold me back with feelings—in order to get it. I knew that whatever it was I felt for Tessa, I could never feel for Camryn.

CHAPTER THIRTY-FOUR

TESSA

I IGNORED HIM ALL DAY. When he asked if I wanted to get lunch, I merely shrugged. I couldn't bring myself to conjure words that didn't include colorful language, and I knew that once I spoke, I'd start to cry, which was something I did not want to do in the office. The sight of Camryn there, her comment about the wedding dress, the long meeting between her, Rowan, and Alistair about the contract . . . it was too much.

The entire time they were locked in that office, I had an incessant burning feeling in my esophagus. Around three thirty, when he was on a call with a factory, I scribbled a note that read: *"Good luck and congratulations. I'm finished with the job, so you won't have to pick me up for work tomorrow,"* and then I walked out of the building and climbed into the Uber with tears in my eyes. I stopped by the art gallery and signed off on the papers for Freddie. It was all a blur. I was the worst person he could have sent to sign those papers because I could've sold his soul to the devil and not known it.

It was five o'clock by the time I took another Uber home, still in a daze. When I reached my house, the *for sale* sign, which had been there for days, made me cry harder, and lastly, the sight of the beat-up old truck in my driveway made me cry even more. I wiped my face as I reached Rowan, who was standing by the front door with his hands in his pockets.

"I drove it over myself. I wanted to make sure . . ." He stopped talking, his brows pinching when he took in my state. He ran down the steps and reached me. "What happened? What's wrong?"

"Nothing." I shook my head, swallowing past the large lump in my throat. Tears swarmed again. I shook my head once more and blinked. "God. I think you were right. I really am afraid of change."

My words came out whispered and horse, and when he wrapped his arms around me, I started crying into his shirt. "Oh, Tessa," he said, running his fingers through my hair soothingly, which only made me cry harder. He held me tighter, as if he were afraid of letting me go. Once I calmed down, he put his lips to my forehead and told me to open the door so we could go inside.

"I have to go get my car," he said. "I left it parked at the shop."

"I'll take you."

"No." He walked into the kitchen and left me standing in the foyer. I followed him when I heard the cabinets open and close, open and close. "You don't have tea?"

"I hate tea."

"Well, I'm going to go get you some tea. You should go upstairs and draw a bath. It'll help you calm down."

"I don't need to calm down." Tears sprung to my eyes again. God, I was being insane. "What is wrong with me?"

"Change is wrong with you." He gave me a small, lopsided smile. I covered my face and cried into my hands. I'd miss his smile so much.

"I don't want you to marry her," I said.

"That's what this is about?"

I nodded as I wiped my tears and sniffled. "Just . . . everything, but that's part of it. I don't want you to marry her. Not *her*."

"Why not?" He walked over, searching my eyes as he waited for me to speak.

For a moment, I wondered how much of what I wanted to say would change his mind. I wondered how much weight my thoughts had at all. Could I change his mind? Would he let me? Would he consider asking me instead of her? Probably not. Maybe it was me. Maybe he didn't want to marry me at all, even under fake circumstances. I thought about Celia and her warning. I'd be stuck here forever. My heart stopped for a moment as I considered that. No. God, no. I couldn't do that. I had goals and dreams that were taking me far away from here. Yes, staying would require less change than my goals. It sounded less scary than moving to Paris or even New York. I swallowed all the words I thought about saying.

"She's an awful human being," I said instead.

His expression softened as he reached me, cupping my face with his hand. He looked at me like I mattered. Like I was the only one. In that moment, I forgot how to breathe. I considered going for it, telling him how I really felt. Telling him I'd do it . . . that I'd marry him if all he needed was a stupid contract. I opened my mouth to say it but couldn't seem to get the words out. He lowered his face and pressed his lips on mine. It was a gentle kiss that spoke of longing and left me bereft when it ended. He looked at me for a long moment, still holding my cheek in his large hand.

"I'm sorry she bothers you."

His flippancy made my jaw clench. "You're sorry she bothers me? Are you kidding? You're really going to fucking marry her, aren't you?"

"It's only a contract."

White-hot rage swelled inside me. I yanked his hand from my face and took a step back. "This is going to ruin your life."

He shrugged. "It's just business."

"She said something about seeing my wedding dress designs. That isn't just business."

His jaw ticked. There was a sudden change in his expression. "When did she say this?"

"Today at the office. She was all smug about it." My voice lowered to a near-mutter, but the rage didn't disappear as I pictured her stupid face and her stupid smile and her stupid words. "I hate her."

"Tess." He sighed heavily.

"Don't 'Tess' me. This isn't high school." I walked to the cupboard and pulled out a glass, unscrewing the bottle I'd corked the other night, and served myself a glass. It was one of the better red wines from the chateau.

Thinking about that place brought another wave of anger. My mother leaving my father and going to live with a man-child. Fucking ridiculous. The entire universe was playing a seriously sick prank on me. I focused on Camryn and continued my rant. "She's such a bitch. Like seriously. Why would you ever marry her? She's a viper and a disgusting excuse for a human being and she's going to make you more miserable than you already are."

I gulped the wine and looked over at him. He looked completely amused, with his arms crossed and his brows raised.

"You done insulting her?"

I set my glass down with a loud clink. "Oh, fuck you."

I walked out of the kitchen and stomped up to my room. I couldn't understand why he didn't see it. She was terrible for him, just a contract or not. She wanted to wear my dress design? She wanted to . . . oh my god.

I felt sick.

He was really going to marry her. Rowan Hawthorne was going to marry another woman, and there wasn't a thing I could do about it. The reality of the situation shook a new wave of emotions into me. I went over to the little bench by the window, the one I'd sat on countless nights when I felt lost and afraid. I slid my shoes off, brought my legs up, and wrapped my arms around them, placing my chin on my knees. Maybe he'd go get his stupid car and leave me alone. Maybe I would draw a bath and drink the rest of that wine and call it a night. I'd pack tomorrow, leave the next day, and never look back. I'd be in New York on Monday, in Paris by Wednesday. I'd let him get married and live happily ever after with that stupid, gold-digging whore.

I jolted a little when he sat by my feet, offering me a new glass of wine. I took it and sipped.

"I don't want you to marry her." My gaze found his. I fought the tears.

"I know."

"But you're going to anyway."

"What do you suggest I do, Tessa?"

I shrugged, biting my lip to keep from shouting, "*Marry me!*" I wouldn't say it, but from the way his eyes widened, I felt like he could read them on my face anyway.

"I would never ask you to stay."

"I know." I hated that about him. Hated that he wouldn't ask. "Because you're scared."

His eyes flashed. He took a sip of wine and merely nodded. Shock shot through me. He was scared. I'd been right all along. We were both scared. I reminded myself of that. I didn't want to give up my goals and dreams, but he understood where I stood on that. He'd never stop me from chasing them. This wasn't high school or college. I wasn't afraid to stay and fight his demons with him like I was back then when I didn't follow him to Columbia. I had my own hurdles to get over. Maybe we could do it together. I licked my lips.

"We can be scared together," I whispered.

"Absolutely not." His voice was firm, leaving little wiggle room for an argument, but I pushed.

"I'm not ready to let go."

"You have to."

"I can't."

"Your wings aren't clipped, and I won't be the reason you start thinking you can't fly," he whispered, coming closer, his wine-infused breath mingling with mine. "You can fly, you know?"

"I know I can. I want to fly with you."

"You aren't a duck."

I smiled despite myself. Bastard. I hated that he made me smile in times like these. "I can be."

"You're too beautiful to be a duck." He kissed the tip of my nose.

"Right, but not too beautiful to not be a fairy."

"With beautiful magic," he answered. My heart pounded. I didn't like this. I couldn't handle this. I looked away, and he kissed my cheek, my jaw. "Magic that pulls me under. My little Sprite with the beautiful golden skin and the amazing dark eyes that could convince a man of anything."

"Stop," I whispered.

He didn't stop. He took our glasses and set them aside. He undressed me in silence, pressing his lips on my chest with each button he undid. Each kiss filled me with an insatiable longing that threatened to rip me apart.

"You're so beautiful, Tessa." He breathed the words, peeling off my skirt, my underwear, unclasping my bra as he sucked my neck, as he let the straps fall from my shoulders. He brought his calloused thumbs and dragged them against my nipples in a motion I felt straight between my legs. I threw my head back and whispered his name.

His mouth came up to my ear, promises falling from his lips. "I'm going to make you scream that tonight."

My heart jackhammered as I undressed him, my fingers not moving fast enough on the buttons of his shirt. He shushed me and put his hands over mine, helping me undo the buttons. My gaze came up to meet his, breath hitching at the expression he had on his face. I stopped unbuttoning. I couldn't do this. I couldn't go through with this. Not tonight. Not like this. Not with him looking at me like that.

"What's on your mind, baby?" he whispered against my lips before kissing me. I softened against him, continued working buttons free as his tongue worked on mine.

"What's on yours?" I countered when I came up for air. I threaded our fingers together and held our hands at our sides, leaning in to place my lips against the center of his chest and drop kisses over his ridged stomach. My tongue peeked out and licked one side of that sensual, deep V that sloped from his hips and disappeared toward my destination. I wasted no time undoing his belt and pulling his pants and briefs down to reveal his proud, thick length. My breath hitched, my insides contracting with memories of it inside me. Without another thought, I took him into my mouth, swirled my tongue around him, moaned around him as his fingers dug into my hair. He wrapped a handful of hair around his hand and pulled me away, bringing me up so I was eye level to his throat before lowering his lips to mine.

I felt the kiss down to my marrow. It was slow and sensual, deep and amorous. Things I'd never felt, never imagined feeling in my lifetime. His hand explored my body, my breasts, the slope of my hips, caressed my inner thighs until it found my core. His fingers were slow, his strokes meaningful against my slippery desire. With each touch, he made me feel everything. I felt exposed and raw, delicate. When he laid me down on my back and looked at me, his hands running over me softly, as if I were something to be cherished, his gaze unblinking from mine, as if I were special, I felt I might just break. He lowered his lips to mine again, captured my emotion in his mouth as he parted my legs and thrust into me. It was a deep, merciless thrust that took my breath with it.

This wasn't fucking.

It wasn't what we'd done before. It didn't feel casual or like something we'd walk away from unscathed. It was daunting and intimidating, a tangled mess of want and need and all the unspoken words weighing heavy between us. My bones rattled with the awareness of him and the pleasure coursing through me.

"I do not bleed," he whispered against me. A reminder not to lose himself, I was sure. I told myself the same thing, but I didn't feel it, didn't believe it. He opened his eyes and looked at me before saying it again. I panted, wanted to call his bluff, but couldn't bring myself to humiliate him like that. Couldn't bring myself to point out that neither of us would be the same after this.

CHAPTER THIRTY-FIVE

HE WAS GONE the following morning, which didn't surprise me in the least. What was surprising was the gaping hole my chest suddenly had in it. By twelve o'clock, when I realized he wasn't outside by the canoes or coming back or even going to call, I packed my bag for New York. My interview wasn't for another two days, but I could definitely do with some fresh air and some Halal Guys. Anything to get away from the memory of Rowan and the way I felt without him. This was exactly what I told myself I did not want. I did not want to be the girl who made decisions because of some man. I wanted to be free of those things, otherwise, I would have followed him to college. My chest hurt when I thought about that. Following him to college hadn't been the answer, I knew that, but a part of me wondered how different things would have been. Would we still be together? Would we have moved back home and started a family instead of where we ended up: him taking over his family's company and me going away for an apprenticeship?

Sulking and digging into the past were stupid notions that offered no real solutions. That was what I told myself during the three-hour car ride to New York. But then, I'd looked out the window and saw things that reminded me of the short road trip I'd taken with Rowan, and I felt like crying. I decided I'd done too much crying yesterday and wiped the tear away before taking a breath, keeping my eyes on the road ahead. To pass the time, I made a mental checklist of all the things I hated about Rowan: he's a control freak, he thinks he's always right, he always has to get the last word, his smile has gotten him further in the world than I ever could go without showing some skin. I'd seen that smile get him out of a traffic ticket on more than one occasion. Something that would never happen to me unless I was wearing a revealing top. He had the body of a god, and I wasn't just saying that because I was in lust with him. He really looked as if he'd been etched by Auguste Rodin himself. He went around in circles until he could convince you to say yes. He had bedroom eyes and used them to his favor. His workspace was meticulous, and who the hell used a Rolodex anymore? He had a way of looking amused by things that weren't the least bit amusing.

By the time I pulled up to the hotel, I'd come up with at least twenty things I did not like about Rowan. There were so many items on that list that I knew I didn't have to even start on a list of things I did like. My phone buzzed just as I closed the door to my room, and I hated myself a little for the way I scrambled to pull the phone from my purse.

When I saw that it was my grandmother calling, disappointment filtered through me. We spoke for a couple of minutes and hung up. I thought about going to bed, sulking the rest of the night, but then I remembered I'd made a few contacts during my trip with Rowan. On a whim, I decided to email Cody, the buyer from Barneys I'd met at the cocktail party with Rowan. He replied instantly, asking if I was free for dinner, and once we'd set it up, I took a quick shower and headed out.

By seven, Rowan still hadn't called, and I was sure he wouldn't. I was so angry with him that I turned off my phone the moment I spotted Cody waiting for me at the restaurant. I walked over with a smile and sat across from him. He was dressed impeccably in a navy suit with a checkered shirt and a tie that I would have never in a million years paired with it, but it looked perfect on him. I said as much, which made him laugh.

"When you work in fashion, you learn to step your game up," he said. "What about you? Have you started your apprenticeship?"

"That's actually what I'm here for. I have my interview tomorrow."

"Are you nervous, excited, ready to get it over with?"

I laughed. "All three, actually."

We ordered our food and drinks and went back to our casual conversation. He told me how he chooses what goes into the store and how they have another set of people stage the products, making it seem as if a customer absolutely needs to buy it.

It was intriguing, especially since I'd only spoken to fabric people up until that point. Sure, I knew there was more to the fashion and design world, but I hadn't realized how extensive it was. We finished eating and continued drinking and all of the anxiety from earlier vanished. I was no longer only thinking about Rowan and how much I missed him. I was actively listening to someone else talk about their job and found that I enjoyed it.

"Your boyfriend didn't come with you this time?"

"You mean Rowan?" I put my glass of wine down and looked up in surprise. "He isn't . . . he isn't my boyfriend."

"Oh. I got a vibe."

"Wrong vibe." I tried to laugh it off, but it sounded weak and uncertain.

"I figured with the way he was looking at you and the way you two . . ." He paused, frowning as he tilted his head. "I don't know how to describe it. You just seemed like a couple."

"Oh. Well, no. Definitely not. We're both very anti-relation-ship, I guess you can say."

"Being in love is scary. Best to play things safe."

My heart pounded. I didn't owe this guy anything, but I still found myself saying, "I'm not in love with him."

"I just got out of a four-year relationship," Cody said, taking a sip of his gin. "It was the worst heartache I'd ever experienced. I cursed the whole thing after that. It took me a month to feel like I could get out of my apartment. Two more to look like a human being. Well, basically, it took eight or nine months for me to be myself again. Guess how long it took her to move on."

"I don't know," I whispered, leaning in slightly.

"Three months. I was still trying to be a human being and she was moving on with her boss."

"That sounds awful."

"It was. It still is. I've been trying to move on, but I don't know." He shrugged. "I compare people to her all the time."

"Four years is a long time."

"I don't regret it, though. Not a single day goes by where I regret being with her those four years. I do regret not fighting for her afterward. If I'd told her that I didn't want to split up, maybe we'd still be together. Who knows? The thought was scary back then, but now it seems so stupid."

I swallowed the lump that seemed to be forming in my throat. "Love is terrifying."

"It sure is." He lifted his glass, I lifted mine, and we toasted to that. We changed the subject back to clothing, which I was thankful for, but in the back of my mind, all I could think about was our previous conversation. Was I in love with Rowan? Really in love with him? Was that why I felt so giddy when he was around and so desperately in need of him when he wasn't? Was that why I checked my phone one hundred times even after I'd turned it off for the night? I said goodbye to Cody and went up to my room, my head buzzing with thoughts of love and alcohol.

What was love anyway? Was it falling into the unknown? I lay in bed the rest of the night and thought about it until I finally decided that I was definitely in love with Rowan Hawthorne. I couldn't even think of a time when I hadn't been. I decided then that I'd tell him. Consequences be damned. He needed to know how I felt.

CHAPTER THIRTY-SIX

FROM THE MOMENT I walked into the New York high-rise, I knew I wouldn't take the job. Not because it was too busy or too loud or anything that may scare someone else away, but because it felt cold and dry and stifling. I'd never believed creativity had a home outside our minds. It was something you either had or you didn't. No fancy high-rise was going to change that. Yet, as I looked around, waiting for Traci to call me into her office, I couldn't help but wonder if working there would stifle my creative drive. When my name was called, I gathered my bag, held my portfolio tight, and walked in. I'd already emailed her a copy of the whole thing, but there was something about having a physical thing to show that couldn't be replaced. The secretary signaled for me to go into the office. I let out a breath as I pushed the large stained-glass door open.

Traci was unlike everything outside of her office. She was vibrant, wearing a burnt-orange dress with frills on the sleeves. Her dyed blonde hair was up in a high ballerina bun, and her smile was warm and welcoming.

"Please, sit," she said after shaking my hand firmly. I did and placed the portfolio on the edge of the desk.

"I love your dress." I smiled. "The color is a dream."

"Ah, a girl who notices. Most people are too busy looking out the windows to notice what I'm wearing, which quite frankly worries me since this isn't an architectural firm." Her brows knotted together in a cute pout that made me laugh and feel instantly at ease. "So, we have a lot to talk about."

And talk we did. About everything from school to when I started drawing, where I learned to sketch, and what it was about design that called to me. I answered all of her questions with sincerity and found that Traci was the kind of woman I could be friends with, whether or not she hired me. She let me speak and nodded and rose her eyebrows every so often, as if impressed or interested, encouraging me to keep talking. I told her about Monte Fabrics and my internship at Hawthorne.

"I'll have to look them up," she said. "Especially if they're getting all that exotic fabric."

"Definitely. They're easy to work with, too, and have the bones of a small company but the product of an international one."

"Cute." She smiled and turned the page on my designs. "So, tell me who our competition is. I know we aren't the only ones who want to steal that brain of yours."

"Umm . . ." I paused, unsure whether I should actually say. Did she want to know or was she just making conversation? I decided she had better things to do than make conversation, so I told her. "Prim. I have my interview with them on Wednesday."

"Prim?" Her mouth dropped. "In Paris?"

I nodded slowly, wondering if saying it aloud was a mistake.

"Girl, what are you doing here?" she asked. "I'm serious. I mean, I want you. Fuck, I'll hire you and start the paperwork right now, but Prim? They have the most exclusive apprentice-ship program there is. Trust me, I got turned down three times!"

My heart skittered. "Really? You?"

"Really. Don't get me wrong, everything happens for a reason. I see that now, but damn." She shook her head, mouth still open slightly. "You need to take that apprenticeship. What's stopping you? Family? It sounds like you're ready to start a life somewhere."

"I am. I mean . . . I don't know what's stopping me." It was the truth. My siblings had managed to move on and start their lives without a second thought. I wasn't sure why I was so hesi-tant to do the same.

"Tell you what," Traci said, "you go and take that apprentice-ship in Paris. If you decide you hate it and want to come home, you call me, and I'll find a spot for you here."

"You'd do that?"

She smiled. "It's cute that you think I'm the one doing you a favor and not the other way around."

As soon as I left, I called Celia. She laughed and laughed and laughed.

"Oh my god, Tess, that's huge!"

"I guess. I mean, right? I just . . ." I couldn't even speak. "I'm still shaking."

She laughed again. "I just . . . I knew it. I knew they'd want you! So? Paris?"

"I have to go over there and interview anyway, right?"

"Tessa," she said, her tone suddenly firm and serious. "You are interviewing them. Don't you get it? You are interviewing *them*. Let that sink in for a moment. I'll wait."

I did let it sink in, and it was unreal. I shook my head. No way. I knew I was good, not that a billion others weren't better than I was, but I knew I had something. I had a drive and love for it that not everyone had. And that was the drive and the something that was making Rowan push me off the cliff without attempting to wait for me at the bottom of it.

CHAPTER THIRTY-SEVEN

I WAS SITTING in the coffee shop perfecting the lecture I was going to give Rowan about love, when Samson walked in, his blue tie flying up in the wind as he shut the door. When he spotted me, he frowned and stalked over, looking like a man on a mission. I laughed a little. He'd called me when I was in line getting my coffee and told me not to move until he made it here, and from the looks of it he seriously needed to talk about something.

"You look like a disheveled version of James Bond."

"Yeah, thanks." His brows rose as he sat across from me and clapped his hands together. "We need to talk."

"Did something happen?" I sat up in my seat, bracing myself for health news. He'd been going to doctors lately and running tests and the mere thought of something being wrong with him sent my heart lurching into my throat.

"They're getting married."

"Oh." I let out a semi-relieved breath, but my heart stayed put as I looked down at my empty pad. I didn't need to jot down everything I was going to say to Rowan. I decided to do the one thing I never thought I would. I'd cut myself open and let it all spill out. "He told me."

"No," he said. "Like right now. They're in the courthouse right *now* signing the papers in front of witnesses."

"What?" I blinked up at him, shutting my book with a *thump.* I stood, coffee forgotten.

"It's done," he said. "He's decided."

"No." I shook my head. "He couldn't have just . . . I mean, he can't . . . I have to go down there." I ran outside, down the sidewalk and toward my truck.

"I'll drive," he said, taking the keys from me. "What exactly are you going to go down there for?"

"Why exactly did you come here to tell me that they were getting married?"

"Because I felt you should know. You should find out from me, from Ro, not . . . I don't know. Not from other people."

I felt like my heart was being punched repeatedly. I put my hand on it and pushed it in, massaged it like I'd seen people on television do when they were trying to revive someone. I glanced at Sam as we peeled out of the parking spot.

"Why aren't you there?"

"I didn't want to partake."

"Are both your parents there?"

"And my grandparents. Yeah."

Stupid parents. Stupid grandparents. Stupid fucking Hawthornes. He parked, and we walked into the courthouse. We put our things through the scanner and picked them up on the other side, continuing our quick walk to the marriage certificate area.

"Wait here. I'll find out where they are."

I nodded, heart rattling out of control. I felt sweat break out across my forehead and took a deep breath, wiping my face quickly. What would I say? Would I just barge in there and tell him not to marry her? Would I tell him I loved him? Would I stay and take the New York offer after all? It was the only way this would work out.

If I went to Paris . . .

I massaged my heart again. Oh god. I couldn't do it. I couldn't tell him. I peeked inside the room and saw all couples sitting in front of the little windows, all there to fill out their certificates, probably preparing for the happiest day of their lives. I pondered leaving, running toward the exit and forgetting the whole thing. Then I remembered Grandma Joan and what she'd said about the importance of speaking our feelings. I kept my feet rooted there. I'd stay. I'd wait. I'd tell him. No matter what happened, I'd tell him.

A door down the hall opened, and I picked up my head to look at it. Samson and Rowan strode into the hallway and walked over to me. My gaze locked with Rowan's, and I had my answer before he even made it over to me.

"I need to speak to her," he said without looking to Sam. "Cover for me."

Sam walked away, and Rowan tugged on my hand. I didn't know where he was taking me, but in that moment, as I followed him through the door that led to the stairwell, I knew I'd follow him anywhere – no questions asked. When the door shut behind us, he turned and faced me again. We looked at each other for a moment, my heart beating uncontrollably, itching to get out of its cage. He brought his hand up, the tips of his fingers caressing my face as if to catalogue each feature.

"Rowan," I whispered. His eyes snapped to mine. He took a step toward me, encasing me in his arms, and crashed his lips onto mine in a desperate kiss that spoke of anguish and goodbyes and made tears prick my eyes. When he broke the kiss, I could merely look at him.

"Please don't do it," I whispered.

"Tess—"

"I love you." My voice wavered as I took in the shock in his eyes. My throat ached with the words as I spoke them, but I pushed past the thick emotion that threatened to cut them from coming into fruition. I'd come this far and I wasn't going to let my fear of being turned away interfere with getting the truth out. "I'm pretty sure I've always been in love with you, and maybe I should've followed you to Columbia. I should've jumped and pulled you with me and—"

"Tessa." His mournful plea broke into my sentence. He squeezed his eyes shut, and when he opened them again, I could see the pain in his gaze. I could feel it. I reached up and ran my shaking fingers over his cheek.

"I know you're scared, but so am I."

"No, Tessa," he whispered. "You have Paris."

"I don't care about Paris. I care about you." My words came out broken and felt as choppy as the tears running down my face.

"I'm not going to be the reason you stay here. You'll end up resenting me. How can . . ." He exhaled loudly, shaking his head. "I'm not a lovable person. Don't you see that? Don't you see how miserable your life would be with me? The moment this contract goes through, I'll be on an airplane all the time. There would be little time for you."

"I don't care," I sputtered. I'll take the New York apprentice-ship. I'll drive there every day, I'll—"

"No." He grabbed my arms, held my gaze. "You will not give up Paris for me. Not for anything."

My lip wobbled. "It isn't your choice to make."

"It is. I want you to go. I *need* you to go."

"Why are you doing this?" I pressed my hands on his chest and pushed him back a little. He laced his fingers through mine and brought his forehead to mine, closing his eyes.

"Tena Koe." He exhaled onto me. I exhaled shakily, a new wave of tears breaking free from my lashes and running down my face. "This is what must be done."

"I don't want you to do this," I whispered against his lips. We opened our eyes, our foreheads still touching, our fingers still laced together. "You're going to ruin everything."

"But not you. I won't ruin you."

"You have ruined me."

"You'll live." He smiled slightly, but I could see the sadness in his eyes. "You'll go to Paris and live out your dream, and I'll be here, rooting you on from afar. You'll be the best designer to come out of this town, and I'll be so damn proud to say I had you in my life once."

I shook my head. "No."

"Yes." He pressed his lips softly against mine.

"I'm in love with you, Rowan."

"You can't be, Sprite."

"Stop saying that." I hiccupped, trying to fight the tears, but they just kept coming. I was cutting myself open for him, and he wasn't responding the way I wanted him to respond. "I love you."

He brought his hands up to cup my face, brushing my tears with his thumbs. "You terrify me. Don't you see that? You fucking terrify me."

It was the first time I realized that ending up with the person you were in love with was a gift. A gift we wouldn't be given. Even as the thought tore me apart, I grabbed his face and kissed him, hoping to breathe enough of my love into him for him to feel it, wishing it would change his mind. That I would talk him out of it so that we could be together. Really together. Instead, he broke the kiss slowly and held my face in his.

"Fly, little Sprite. Flap those beautiful, magical wings and fly."

He let go. The door rattled with his exit, but I was unable to make myself move. He'd left me with my chest ripped open and my heart in my hands.

CHAPTER THIRTY-EIGHT

ROWAN

"DUDE. She told you she loves you," my brother said beside me.

I'd left Tessa in the stairwell and made my way to the men's bathroom, which was where he had found me with my face buried into my hands like I was breathing into a paper bag. She'd opened herself to me so completely, and I'd turned my back on her. I wanted to give in to the rage that flowed through my veins, wanted to punch something and take my anger out on the world. Instead, I waited. I calmed myself. I tried to summon all the words my father had repeated to me when I was a child and found I couldn't think of any.

I only came to the conclusion that, at some point, I had to grow up and stop pointing the finger at the person I wanted to blame for my own fuck ups. I had to accept my own mistakes. Maybe this was my moment to do that. But I felt like shit.

"Ro?" Samson said, tentative as he stood beside me.

I heard him but couldn't find it in me to react. I just stood there, face in hands. I wanted the day to pass. Wanted the stupid fake ceremony to go on without me. My brother put a hand on my shoulder. I nearly flinched but forced myself to stand still.

"You need to calm down," he said. "You're shaking."

"Why would she tell me those things?" I focused on breathing. In and out. In and out. "She knew I needed to do this, and she came down here and fucked with my head. Why would she do that?"

"Did she fuck with your head?"

I dropped my hands and looked at my brother. "Obviously."

His eyes widened as he took in my appearance. I didn't know what I looked like, but if it was an ounce of how I felt, I must have been a mess. "Maybe we should postpone this."

"There's no point. It needs to be done."

"Maybe you should let me do it," he said. "I'd let you run the company anyway."

In theory, it was a great idea, but I didn't want that for my little brother. Differences or no differences, Samson didn't deserve that life. The only thing he'd ever asked for was to have room for his creativity. Doing this would stifle that, and I couldn't bear it. I swallowed down the knot in my throat, the one throbbing and reminding me about the woman I just let walk away. The one I would from this day forward only be able to summon in dreams when I closed my eyes at night. I'd never feel her hand in mine or her heart beating against my own. I'd never see those beautiful almond eyes light up when she smiled, or feel her smooth skin beneath mine. I shook my head and looked at my brother.

"When I thought you two were dating, I was furious," I said. "Because she's mine, always has been, and I wanted her to myself. Maybe that's a dick thing to say, but it's true. More than anything, I was mad because I thought being with you would hinder her growth. She needs to get out of here. She deserves to do something for herself for once."

He looked at me for a moment, seemingly stunned. "You love her."

I scoffed, but it sounded weak in my ears. "Please. I don't even know what love is."

"I don't either, but if I had to make a bet, I'd bet it was this— letting go of someone with the knowledge that you'd be miserable without them. You say you're selfish, but you're doing the selfless thing here."

"It doesn't feel like I am." It felt like I was breaking apart at the seams.

He let out a breath, watched me closely, and finally, opened his arms and hugged me. I closed my eyes and hugged him back. Was losing a loved one what it took for two people who loved each other to find themselves back to each other? I wasn't sure, but I couldn't remember the last time we'd hugged. I thought about Tessa and how alone she must have felt in that moment. I dropped my arms and swallowed the lump in my throat. My brother wiped his face quickly.

"You have to go find her," I said. "I don't want her driving right now."

"I will." He slapped my shoulder and walked away, turning toward me one last time. "It's only four years, right? The contract."

"Four long years." Thanks to Camryn's clause that she wouldn't bear children, we were able to keep a limited contract.

The goal was that by year three or four I would be able to buy out the board and change the company name and all of its information so that my uncle couldn't come back and sue for it.

"You've suffered worse." He shrugged, shot me a small smile, and left.

I stayed a moment longer, washed my face, my hands, gripped the sink and looked at my reflection in the mirror. I tried to summon those words my father said to me again, but the only thing I could think was what a liar he was, even as I opened my mouth to say it, what came out was different from what I had rehearsed countless times before.

"I bleed."

I bleed.

I bleed.

CHAPTER THIRTY-NINE

TESSA

I STAYED LONG ENOUGH to see him walk into the room and then a little longer just in case. I shouldn't have. I knew that. I just wanted to make sure he wasn't lying. I wanted to make sure that if he bolted and ran out the door, I was right there waiting. It would have been lovely, but this wasn't a movie and no one was coming out of that door. Still. I stared at it extra hard, willing his presence.

"Hey."

I jumped, pressing a hand to my heart. "Jesus, Sam."

"We should go," he said, putting his hand on my forearm and tugging me lightly. I let him. The high of adrenaline that had been coursing through me a short while ago was wearing off quickly, and I found myself feeling the aftermath of it—a drunken-like exhaustion replacing it all. My knees wobbled. Sam held me tighter, wrapped an arm around me as we walked from the building.

"You okay?"

I nodded. I wasn't, but I nodded. Sometimes it was better to live in a lie than accept reality. He drove me home in silence. When he pulled up to the house, he parked and walked me to the front door.

"You sure you want to stay here all alone?"

Another nod. "I have to finish packing."

"Maybe you should stay with Joan tonight."

"No." I offered a shake of my head instead of a nod this time. "I need to finish packing."

"Okay. I'll stay a little while if you don't mind. Make some tea or something."

I shrugged as I unlocked the door.

"Still no offers?"

"I don't know. Dad's handling it now. I gave the realtor his number." I started to walk upstairs. "Make yourself at home."

I shut the bedroom door behind me. My knees went weak again. I wanted to make it all the way to the sitting nook by my window, but I didn't end up making it past my bed before I completely collapsed. I pulled myself up and crawled to my pillow, but the moment my face hit the soft fabric, I smelled him and lost it. Heavy, uncontrollable sobs rocked through me and turned into a near wail. I never really had him to begin with, but I still felt his absence everywhere, and I'd just said goodbye. I registered my door opening. I wasn't sure how long I'd been crying, but when I saw Samson and Grandma Joan beside him, I lost it all over again. She rushed to my side and wrapped her arms around me.

"Oh, honey." She shushed and rocked me like she did when I was a child. I couldn't stop shaking against her.

"I . . . I . . . I . . . t-t-t-told him a-a-a-and he j-j-just . . ."

"Shh. I know. I know." She caressed my hair softly, letting my cry onto her chest. I felt like with every breath my sob may lessen, but instead it grew with each thought, each memory, each realization, that this was really happening. He wasn't coming. He really wasn't coming.

CHAPTER FORTY

TESSA

One month later . . .

GRANDMA JOAN and Samson had flown with me to Paris, whether it had been to make sure I actually took the trip or to catch me if I fell, I didn't know. Grandma Joan said it was because my mom wanted her to visit. She wasn't thrilled about it and said she didn't want to see my mother canoodling with a child. She'd actually used the word "canoodling." As it turned out, Mom's new boyfriend was older than Freddie. Not by much, but older nonetheless. Sam used the trip as a way to clear his mind. He hadn't been feeling well either, and didn't want to be home while all the fighting was going on. We'd stayed at the Chateau that first weekend and took the train to Paris on Sunday. Sam had a flight to catch Monday, and I had my apprenticeship at Prim, which I'd accepted.

I stopped crying on the fifth day. Or maybe it was the sixth. I had a perfectly beautiful studio apartment with a lovely view of the Eiffel that was only a few blocks from Prim. Despite the cold I couldn't seem to kick and the way my heart felt like it was going through a grinder every time I thought about Rowan, which was every night, but I'd managed to keep my head straight and pay attention to all the things I was being taught during training.

My mild cold grew into the flu, which came with the worst nasal headaches ever. By my third Friday at work, my new boss, Yamira, gave me a warm wine to try.

"Just drink it and relax this weekend," she'd said. "Instead of exploring the city, order in. You'll have plenty of time to explore once you feel better."

I took the wine gratefully and went home with every intention of unwinding. That was, until I checked my email and saw a message from Rowan. Every nerve in my body contracted as I clicked it and opened it to find pictures. Not just any pictures. Wedding pictures, which appeared to have been taken in Rogers Williams Park. His face was stoic in all of them. That was the one thing that made me not want to hurl my tablet. I'd told him how I felt and it hadn't worked out quite the way I'd planned, but I didn't regret it for a moment. I'd cried for him, for the loss of what could have been, but I was fine. I'd been completely fine up until I saw the pictures, but as I clicked through them because, of course, I had to click through them, I zoomed in on her dress, and my blood went cold.

I knew that dress.

I'd looked at that design countless times before trashing it because the ends of the sleeves were too pointy for the lacy material I'd intended it for. And there was Camryn, blonde, skinny, supermodel-like Camryn, wearing *my* scrap work. How did she find that? Where did she find that? I racked my memory, trying to figure it out until I realized—the coffee shop. He must have taken the paper, folded it into his pocket, and kept it.

Did he think this was flattering? Having his new wife use a dress I designed? A strange ache developed deep inside me. I dropped my tablet, brought one hand to my mouth and the other over my stomach in hopes that I wouldn't be sick all over the living room. My gaze found the tablet where it had landed face up on the rug, and my heart pounded erratically against my ribs as I stared at the picture. Her ring looked huge. She probably picked it out herself. Was he wearing a ring? I covered my mouth harder, fighting the revulsion that threatened to pour out of me. Once I had been sure I wouldn't throw up, I scooped up the tablet, wrote him an email telling him to go fuck himself, and turned the thing off. Surprisingly, it only took me a few days to get over it. Normally, it would've taken longer. Maybe it was the city, the lights, and the romanticism about it, but Paris seemed to be good for my soul.

That had been three weeks ago, and I hadn't heard from him since. A few hours ago, I'd forced myself to finally go sit at the doctor's office that Yamina recommended and got a full checkup. I explained to them my symptoms, what I'd taken, which wasn't much aside from warm wine, and I waited. Waited. In the end, they told me I had the flu and sent me home with a Z pack. I went to the little pharmacy in the corner of my apartment and stood in line waiting to fill the antibiotics, grabbed some things I thought of last minute, and went home.

When I got home, I curled up on the couch, arms wrapped around my legs, feeling like utter shit, thinking about the damn dress and Rowan, until a knock on my door pulled out of my funk. I stood quickly, the dreamer in me envisioning Rowan on the other side of it, kneeling and groveling for forgiveness. Forgiveness I'd still give to him if he asked.

What I found when I opened the door was Celia. All the sobs I'd already gotten passed came rushing back at the sight of her. We threw our arms around each other. I cried, and she held me the way only a sister can. Then she dropped her hands and, like only a sister can, gave me a rigorous inspection I clearly did not pass.

"You look like shit."

"I feel like shit." I sniffled, wiping my face. "I didn't know you were coming."

"Surprises aren't meant to be announced." She smiled, picked up her duffel bag, and walked inside. "Cute place." She walked around, light on her feet, bouncing from here to there, her long, black hair swishing with each movement. "Really cute place," she added as she pulled the curtains back and saw the Eiffel.

"I know. You want anything? I don't have much."

She waved a hand, turned those warm brown eyes back to mine. "You aren't playing hostess. I'm here to take care of you. What's going on?"

And I told her. I told her about Rowan, which she knew about. I told her about the email and the dress and everything that was on my mind. I told her that most of all, I missed him. I missed his arms and his scent and his warmth and the way his eyes lit up when he was going to say something he knew would make me want to punch him. And between it all, I cried and sniffled.

"Sorry. I thought I was done crying."

"Don't be sorry." She put a hand on my shoulder and then dropped it, her face contorting with confusion and anger. "He fucking sent you their wedding pictures? Why the hell would he do that?"

"Not wedding pictures. They got married in court. This was a photoshoot they had recently." I tried to shrug it off nonchalantly, but felt a new wave of tears fill my eyes as I thought about the pictures. "Probably because they were going to be printed in some publication and he wanted me to see them first."

"She copied your dress design, though? You can sue for that."

"It isn't like it was . . ." I shook my head, too weary to explain copyright laws and things of that nature. I'd looked it all up and came up with the conclusion that nothing could be done. What was the point of trying? "Whatever. It isn't like the fabric was right for the design and the lace up top didn't fall over her shoulders like it should have. It wasn't my best design."

"Still," she said and sighed, turning her lithe body toward mine. "Have you taken the meds?"

"Not yet." I pointed at the bag on the counter. She stood up, walked over to her duffel bag and crouched down to open the zipper.

"Don't be mad."

"What did you do now?" I sighed, thinking about the time she bought me a bouquet of daffodils because she'd forgotten I was allergic to it. She couldn't possibly have flowers in there though. Instead, she fished out a pregnancy kit. My jaw dropped.

"What is that for?"

"For you because we need to get to the bottom of this."

"Oh my god, Celia, you're being ridiculous." I stood quickly and walked to the kitchen, taking the meds out of the bag. "This is all I need."

"Just. Please," she said, waving the box around. I rolled my eyes and took it because I knew my sister. She'd go on and on about this if I didn't comply. I pulled my hair into a messy bun and ripped the box open, taking out the stick. Unease rolled through me as I looked at it. How many women had looked at this very thing and wished for things, or not wished for things. I wasn't entirely sure what side I fell on. I'd landed the apprenticeship of my dreams and was striving.

"What is happening?" Celia asked, saying the words slowly as I flushed the toilet.

"I'm not pregnant." I set the test down beside me as I washed my hands.

"It was that fast?"

"No. I'm just telling you what I know. I have the flu."

"Tessa." It was her warning tone. Her mouth was slightly parted, eyes wide as she stood over the stick. "I am seriously freaking the fuck out now. I mean, seriously, I fucking . . . I mean, Jesus. I'm at a loss for words! When am I ever at a loss for words?"

"Hopefully soon," I grumbled, walking out of the bathroom. She followed, picking up the stick with two fingers, as if afraid being pregnant—which I absolutely was not—could rub off on her, placed it on the coffee table and sat on one side. I sat beside her, watching the stick.

"You probably shouldn't take whatever antibiotics they prescribed if this is positive," she said. "Oh my god, what if this is positive?"

My stomach squeezed. "It won't be positive. It's been like, forever."

"Still." She looked as if she were having difficulty breathing. "Oh my god, Tess."

"Shut up, Celia. Just shut up."

We both sat at the edge of our seats, eyeing the stick, which was developing some kind of line.

"Did you read the instructions?"

I glared at her. "No, asshole. Didn't you? You had the box while I was peeing on the stick."

She jumped from the couch and sprinted to the box, bringing

it back with her. She looked between the instructions and the stick, eyes mega-wide.

"What?" My heart dropped.

Her gaze lifted to mine, eyes still wide. "Holy fuck."

"No." I took the stick in my hand, snatched the box from hers, and compared them. "No."

"Tess," she whispered. "I think you're pregnant."

I shut my eyes, clutching the stick and box in my hands. My knees buckled and seemed to unscrew completely before I landed on the couch with an *oomph*.

READ THE CONCLUSION IN MY WAY
BACK TO YOU -

My Way Back to You

CPSIA information can be obtained
at www.ICGtesting.com
Printed in the USA
LVHW04s1300161018
593788LV00001B/185/P